Acting Edition

The Refuge Plays

**Protect the Beautiful Place
Walking Man
Early's House**

by Nathan Alan Davis

SAMUEL FRENCH

Protect the Beautiful Place, Walking Man, Early's House
Copyright © 2024 by Nathan Alan Davis
All Rights Reserved

THE REFUGE PLAYS is fully protected under the copyright laws of the United States of America, the British Commonwealth, including Canada, and all member countries of the Berne Convention for the Protection of Literary and Artistic Works, the Universal Copyright Convention, and/or the World Trade Organization conforming to the Agreement on Trade Related Aspects of Intellectual Property Rights. All rights, including professional and amateur stage productions, recitation, lecturing, public reading, motion picture, radio broadcasting, television, online/digital production, and the rights of translation into foreign languages are strictly reserved.

ISBN 978-0-573-71130-5

www.concordtheatricals.com
www.concordtheatricals.co.uk

FOR PRODUCTION INQUIRIES

UNITED STATES AND CANADA
info@concordtheatricals.com
1-866-979-0447

UNITED KINGDOM AND EUROPE
licensing@concordtheatricals.co.uk
020-7054-7298

Each title is subject to availability from Concord Theatricals Corp., depending upon country of performance. Please be aware that *THE REFUGE PLAYS* may not be licensed by Concord Theatricals Corp. in your territory. Professional and amateur producers should contact the nearest Concord Theatricals Corp. office or licensing partner to verify availability.

CAUTION: Professional and amateur producers are hereby warned that *THE REFUGE PLAYS* is subject to a licensing fee. The purchase, renting, lending or use of this book does not constitute a license to perform this title(s), which license must be obtained from Concord Theatricals Corp. prior to any performance. Performance of this title(s) without a license is a violation of federal law and may subject the producer and/or presenter of such performances to civil penalties. Both amateurs and professionals considering a production are strongly advised to apply to the appropriate agent before starting rehearsals, advertising, or booking a theatre. A licensing fee must be paid whether the title(s) is presented for charity or gain and whether or not admission is charged. Professional/Stock licensing fees are quoted upon application to Concord Theatricals Corp.

This work is published by Samuel French, an imprint of Concord Theatricals Corp.

No one shall make any changes in this title(s) for the purpose of production. No part of this book may be reproduced, stored in a retrieval system, scanned, uploaded, or transmitted in any form, by any means, now known or yet to be invented, including mechanical, electronic, digital, photocopying, recording, videotaping, or otherwise, without the prior written permission of the publisher. No one shall share this title(s), or any part of this title(s), through any social media or file hosting websites.

For all inquiries regarding motion picture, television, online/digital and other media rights, please contact Concord Theatricals Corp.

MUSIC AND THIRD-PARTY MATERIALS USE NOTE

Licensees are solely responsible for obtaining formal written permission from copyright owners to use copyrighted music and/or other copyrighted third-party materials (e.g. artworks, logos) in the performance of this play and are strongly cautioned to do so. If no such permission is obtained by the licensee, then the licensee must use only original music and materials that the licensee owns and controls. Licensees are solely responsible and liable for clearances of all third-party copyrighted materials, including without limitation music, and shall indemnify the copyright owners of the play(s) and their licensing agent, Concord Theatricals Corp., against any costs, expenses, losses and liabilities arising from the use of such copyrighted third-party materials by licensees. For music, please contact the appropriate music licensing authority in your territory for the rights to any incidental music.

IMPORTANT BILLING AND CREDIT REQUIREMENTS

If you have obtained performance rights to this title, please refer to your licensing agreement for important billing and credit requirements.

SPECIAL THANKS

Thank you, Patricia McGregor. Your artistry and advocacy over the course of many years are an indelible part of *The Refuge Plays*. This story has always been as close to your heart as it is to my own, and I will be ever thankful for your friendship and the work we were able to do together on these plays.

Thank you to the many people who stepped forward to support this project in its long development journey, including Kelly Miller, Jesse Cameron Alick, Jack Phillips Moore, Anna Morton Stacey, Emily Mann, Branden Jacobs-Jenkins, and Lucas McMahon.

Thank you to all the actors who lent their artistry to these plays in readings and workshops over the years, especially Jessica Frances Dukes, Lizan Mitchell, Sekou Laidlow, and Amanda Warren, who were among the most frequent collaborators.

Thank you to New York Theatre Workshop, my artistic home, for always surrounding me with kindness and moral support.

Thank you to the late Todd Haimes, who said yes to this enormous project during a time of great uncertainty and contraction in our industry.

Thank you to the late Jim Houghton, who had the foresight to send the early drafts of *The Refuge Plays* to Patricia, and set us on the path.

TABLE OF CONTENTS

Part 1: Protect the Beautiful Place 1

Part 2: Walking Man 73

Part 3: Early's House 141

Part 1:
Protect the Beautiful Place

PART 1: PROTECT THE BEAUTIFUL PLACE was originally commissioned by The Public Theater (Oskar Eustis, Artistic Director; Patrick Willingham, Executive Director) as part of the Gail Merrifield Papp Fellowship. It was originally produced in New York City by Roundabout Theatre Company in association with New York Theatre Workshop at the Harold and Miriam Steinberg Center for Theatre / Laura Pels Theatre on October 11, 2023. The performance was directed by Patricia McGregor, with set design by Arnulfo Maldonado, lighting design by Stacey Derosier, costume design by Emilio Sosa, and original music and sound design by Marc Anthony Thompson. The production stage manager was Katie Ailinger. The cast was as follows:

GAIL	Jessica Frances Dukes
EARLY	Nicole Ari Parker
WALKING MAN	Jon Michael Hill
JOY	Ngozi Anyanwu
HA-HA	J.J. Wynder-Wilkins
SYMPHONY	Mallori Taylor Johnson

CHARACTERS

GAIL – (W, 60s) The de facto head of the household.
EARLY – (W, 80s) The original matriarch of this family.
WALKING MAN – (M, 60s) A ghost. Gail's husband. Early's son.
JOY – (W, 30s) Gail and Walking Man's daughter.
HA-HA – (M, 17) Joy's son.
SYMPHONY – (W, 19) A young woman from a nearby town.

SETTING

A small, makeshift, two-room house, which is nestled deep in a southern Illinois forest.

TIME

Fall. The 2010s.

AUTHOR'S NOTE

An ellipsis line in the dialogue [...] represents a pause, a beat, or perhaps a physical action.

When a line of dialogue ends in a dash [–] this means the next line comes right on top of it, perhaps with an overlap.

Where an overlap is needed in a specific place, it is marked by a slash [/].

One

(Starlight shines through a canopy of ancient trees, beneath which is a small, two-room house.)

(A shadowed figure makes his way through the dark and quiet main room. This is **WALKING MAN**.*)*

*(***WALKING MAN** *kisses* **EARLY**, *who is sleeping stretched out in an easy chair.)*

(He kisses **JOY**, *who sleeps on a sofa bed.)*

(He kisses **HA-HA**, *who sleeps in a sleeping bag on the floor.)*

(Also in this main room: a wood-burning stove, a table and chairs, a cupboard, a coat rack, a small bookcase with books.)

(In the bedroom, on a proper bed, **GAIL** *sleeps.)*

*(***WALKING MAN** *approaches the bedroom, but does not enter.)*

(He exits the house, closing the door behind him.)

*(***GAIL** *wakes. She spins herself out of bed, takes a tobacco pipe out of a dresser drawer. She lights it and smokes.)*

GAIL. Rope.

You know about it?

How when you squeezin' it,

When you holdin' somethin' up,

Holdin' up somethin' heavy like a car or a house?

Yeah.

You can *will* yourself to hold on but your hands, they gonna shut down. Stop workin'.

Your will ain't enough.

That's not a pleasant thing to know.

That'll keep you up at night.

(Re: the messy bed.)

I ain't finna make the bed just yet.

This *my* time to do what *I* do.

This time between dawn and sunrise, I stand alone,

And smoke my deadass husband's pipe,

And watch.

When you watch in the dark like this, shapes form, thoughts form,

And thoughts, sooner or later they find their ways, don't they? They find their familiar ways.

Same old thoughts,

Same old *doubts*,

Same old questions swimming around in your heart and they don't never tire out.

…

Did we do the right thing?

Stayin' out here?

Tryna keep ourselves a step to the side of the world?

...

> (*A nod towards the other room.*)

That's my daughter over there,

And my grandson,

And my deadass husband's mother:

It's hard not to love people when they're sleeping.

Not that I *don't* love them when they awake…

It's just that ain't none of 'em capable of holdin' that rope with me.

So you and I can steal this little time, these little minutes.

But when the sun rises, I –

> (*The sun rises.*)
>
> (**GAIL** *smokes as the sky begins to brighten.*)
>
> (*In the main room,* **HA-HA** *sits up.*)
>
> (*He goes to the wood-burning stove and opens it. He looks around, at a loss.*)

HA-HA. Mama?

...

Ain't no wood left.

JOY. Mhmm…

> (**HA-HA** *grabs a coat from the coat rack, slips on a pair of shoes, and exits the house.*)

(**GAIL**, *having finished making her bed, enters the main room.*)

JOY. Morning, Mama.

GAIL. I heard Ha-Ha say there's no wood.

JOY. He went to take care of it.

GAIL. All the wood your daddy chopped is gone?

JOY. Yes, ma'am.

GAIL. *All* of it? You sure?

JOY. Ha-Ha's choppin' up more.

GAIL. Alright, I need to go stop him before he lop off a foot –

JOY. He'll be fine. Daddy taught him how.

GAIL. Walking Man was a terrible teacher.

JOY. Mama.

GAIL. Well, he was. "See how I did that? Now you do it." That ain't teaching.

EARLY. Cold in here.

(**EARLY** *rises and slips on a coat and shoes.*)

JOY. Morning, Grandma Early.

Ha-Ha out getting more wood for the stove.

GAIL. Mornin' Great Grandma, your chair breakin' in okay?

EARLY. Don't be talkin' to me, I need to use the toilet.

(**EARLY** *exits the house.*)

GAIL. ...

Forgot to say good morning to you, Joy. How'd you sleep?

JOY. ...

>   (**JOY** *embraces* **GAIL**, *fully.*)

GAIL. What is it?

JOY. I'm gonna miss you.

GAIL. Where I'm goin'?

JOY. ...

Daddy's been visiting at night –

GAIL. How many times I told you don't listen to your father no more, he's dead –

JOY. He said last night he was gettin' ready to take you with him –

GAIL. Tell him to take his rickety old mother if he *lonely. Please.*

JOY. ...

GAIL. I'm sorry, baby. Grandma Early is not rickety.

Well she *is* rickety, but that don't mean I should be callin' it to attention.

JOY. ...

GAIL. It ain't that I don't still love your daddy. I just get a little frustrated when people try to act like they the Grim Reaper, when they ain't nothin' but a lonely, meddling ghost who needs to stay outa my house so I can get my work done.

Now if Ha-Ha gonna do the wood he need to be a lot quicker than this, it's getting colder by the second. HA-HA!! –

>   (*As* **GAIL** *opens the door to yell to* **HA-HA**, *he comes in with several eggs cradled in his shirt. He places the eggs on the counter, makes a beeline for the bookshelf, and pulls out a book.*)

JOY. Baby, where's the wood?

HA-HA. Great Grandma choppin' the wood.

GAIL. Boy you can't let your great gran chop wood, what's wrong with you!?

HA-HA. She took the axe from me. She said I wasn't doin' it right.

GAIL. ...

HA-HA. I brought in eggs for breakfast.

JOY. ...

HA-HA. I'll go back out.

JOY. Let her tire herself out and then you gotta go straight for her wrist.

HA-HA. Okay, Mama.

JOY. Gotta be decisive now.

HA-HA. Yes, ma'am.

> (*HA-HA goes back outside.*)

> (*GAIL begins preparing the food that HA-HA brought in.*)

JOY. ...

It's made me happy. Daddy coming by.

With Grandma Early getting like she is,

And Ha-Ha – God help me with that boy –

GAIL. He's a good boy.

JOY. I know he is.

GAIL. Uhuh, act like you know, then.

JOY. ...

I'm gonna miss you being around all the time, but please don't make this any harder than it already is.

You can still come visit us at night like Daddy does.

GAIL. I'm not going any damn where.

JOY. I don't know what you so stressed about, I'm the one that's gonna have to hold things down without you.

You taught me death was a comfort.

GAIL. It's a comfort when you old and sick and losing your mind like great grandma lumberjack out there. Not for me. I got *work* to do.

>   (**EARLY** *bursts through the door with two armfuls of chopped firewood. She lays the wood on the floor.*)

>   (**HA-HA** *follows her in with more wood.*)

EARLY. Start that fire now, child.

HA-HA. Okay, great grandma.

>   (**HA-HA** *puts a log in the stove along with some kindling. He lights it.*)

>   (**EARLY** *begins stacking the wood into a pile.*)

JOY. Grandma, don't stack that wood, Ha-Ha got it –

GAIL. Grandma Early, sit down, we'll get you some tea, okay? You want some tea –

EARLY. Not if you makin' it.

You always make it taste sharp.

GAIL. Grandma Early, I don't know what that means.

EARLY. Course you don't know, 'cause meanings escape you. Like a dog lookin' for mice in the morning – you ain't never gonna catch 'em. Cat got 'em. You got to be like the cat. Awake when the food's awake. What have you ever done in your whole life? What have you ever done?

JOY. ...

Mama I'll finish breakfast, why don't you go ahead out and take your shower.

>(**GAIL** *goes into the bedroom, takes clean clothes out of the dresser, and exits the house.*)

>(**EARLY** *sits in her chair.*)

EARLY. That ain't no woman.

JOY. Grandma, that's Gail.

EARLY. I know her name.

JOY. You love Gail.

EARLY. ...

JOY. ...

I'll get your tea.

EARLY. Not sharp please, sweetie.

>(**JOY** *pours water into a kettle, then places the kettle on top of the stove.*)

HA-HA. Want me to do the eggs?

JOY. Yes please, baby.

>(**HA-HA** *takes a pan out of the cabinet, places it on top of the stove and begins cooking the food...*)

EARLY. Who said *baby*?

JOY. I was talkin' to Ha-Ha, Grandma.

EARLY. There's s'pose to be babies in a house.

*(Looking directly at **HA-HA**.)* Where's your babies?

HA-HA. ...

EARLY. Where's your babies?

JOY. Grandma, he's only seventeen.

EARLY. So what? That ain't young. What do people be doin' with they time on earth?

JOY. Set the table please, Ha-Ha.

(**HA-HA** *sets the table.*)

(**HA-HA** *pulls out a book from the bookshelf.*)

JOY. Ha-Ha. You can read after breakfast.

(**HA-HA** *puts the book back on the shelf.*)

(*A short silence.*)

EARLY. Why am I sleepin' on a chair?

And my son is dead and gone and Gail got that big ole bed all to herself.

JOY. Mama offered you the bed a hundred times and you said you wanted the chair –

EARLY. This chair is ugly! I ain't never even heard of a chair this ugly. I heard some scary stories, but ain't never heard of this.

JOY. Grandma Early, that's a perfectly nice chair –

(**GAIL** *enters, now dressed in day clothes.*)

Mama took the truck into town every day for a *month*.

And stood in the parking lot at the mall,

And held a sign,

And waved her arms around for hours and hours and hours,

Just so she could buy you that chair.

That's a nice chair.

…

> (**JOY** *goes to the bedroom dresser, grabs a set of clothes, and exits.*)

EARLY. What did the sign say?

GAIL. It said "Savings, This Way."

EARLY. That's all it said?

GAIL. And it had an arrow.

EARLY. Oh. Well that's good. Arrows are good.

They tell you where you need to go.

GAIL. ...

EARLY. You cross at me, Gail?

GAIL. No, ma'am.

EARLY. Yes you are.

> (**GAIL** *takes the pan off the stove, places it on the table and covers it with a plate.*)

GAIL. Ha-Ha, would you get your great grandma some tea?

HA-HA. Water ain't boiled yet.

GAIL. It's about to, it's plenty hot enough, come get a cup.

EARLY. Why you got to speak to him so harshly? He ain't done a thing to you.

GAIL. ...

Do you think it's hot enough, Ha-Ha?

HA-HA. Yes, ma'am.

GAIL. Go ahead and steep some tea.

And make sure it's not too sharp.

HA-HA. How do I make it not sharp –

GAIL. You gonna have to ask your great grandmother about that, baby.

HA-HA. Great grandma, how do I make it not sharp –

EARLY. It's real simple: Don't pour it sharp, don't stir it sharp, don't be thinkin' daggers into me while you put the honey in.

HA-HA. Okay.

EARLY. *(To* **GAIL.***)* I know why you mad at me.

You mad at me 'cause you gonna die first.

HA-HA. Oh, Grandma Gail I was gonna ask: can I sit next to you at breakfast? Can I switch places with Mama and sit next to you?

GAIL. How come?

HA-HA. 'Cause after you die we're never gonna have breakfast together again.

GAIL. There's no reason to think I'm gonna die soon, Ha-Ha.

EARLY. Yes there is a reason. Walking Man told us. Told all three of us while you was over there rollin' in your meadow of blankets.

GAIL. Walking Man be playing too much, and he don't know when to stop.

(To **HA-HA.***)* You hear that, Ha-Ha? If your grandfather comes into the house again, you tell him to stop playing and send him right back out the door.

HA-HA. …

GAIL. You can't be studying folks that don't know how to act.

And he never has.

Like he was raised by wolves.

EARLY. ...

>(**HA-HA** *gives* **EARLY** *her cup of tea.*)

HA-HA. Here go your tea, great grandma.

EARLY. That smells perfect and I'm sure it's gonna taste perfect. Thank you.

HA-HA. You welcome, great grandma.

...

Gonna read until breakfast.

>(**HA-HA** *takes a book off the shelf.*)
>
>(*He reads.*)

EARLY. What you readin'?

HA-HA. *Invisible Man.*

EARLY. Oh, you readin' Ralph's books, huh?

Gail, how come you ain't tell me?

You goin' into Ralph's books now. Good. Good, good.

Good ole Ralph.

HA-HA. You knew Ralph Ellison, great grandma?

>(**GAIL** *silently shakes her head "no."*)

EARLY. Oh, sure. Still do be knowin' him.

He's tactical, Ralph is.

HA-HA. Tactical?

EARLY. Always.

HA-HA. Like in a battle?

EARLY. Yes indeed.

The great, great battle.

The big one.

What part you in now?

HA-HA. He's drivin' around in the car at the university.

EARLY. Oh, you got such a ways to go. Don't let me stop you.

>   (**HA-HA** *reads.*)

And what you need to do, Ha-Ha: You need to read that whole book. And then you need to turn it back over and read it again.

>   (**HA-HA** *continues to read.*)

GAIL. Ha-Ha.

HA-HA. *(To* **EARLY.***)* Yes ma'am, I will.

>   (*He reads...*)

EARLY. 'Cause Ralph and them, they put they messages in code.

Got to keep reading the code 'til it cracks. 'Til you know what the words are tryin' to say to *you.*

HA-HA. Yes ma'am.

EARLY. That's what the Silent Messenger places in your heart.

Comes shrouded in those syllables like cover of night,

Slips her long fingers through the prison bars of your ribs

And squeezes.

...

Why you think we still here? Huh?

>   (*Firmly pats her chest.*)

EARLY. Ralph's heart to mine.

Harlem ain't no haven.

Chi-town ain't my town.

And college ain't knowledge.

Gotta make your own world in this world 'cause if you don't: the axis is a motherfucker.

Cast your black ass right out into space. Way, way out there where can't *nobody* bring you back.

HA-HA. ...

Yes, ma'am.

> (**JOY** *enters, now dressed in day clothes.*)

JOY. *(To* **HA-HA.***)* Put that book away and go wash up for breakfast.

> (**HA-HA** *puts the book away and moseys toward the bedroom dresser.*)

Quick now, we all waitin'!

> (**HA-HA** *exits the house to wash up.*)

EARLY. You ain't tell me he was reading Ralph.

JOY. Grandma Early he's read that book ten times.

EARLY. ...

Well he don't act like he's read it.

> (**JOY** *and* **GAIL** *plate the food and pour glasses of water from the bucket.*)

GAIL. Grandma Early, can I take your tea to the table?

EARLY. Walking Man was not raised by wolves.

He was raised by me.

And I'm glad he comes to visit at night.

GAIL. May I take your tea to the table?

EARLY. Don't touch it, don't even look at it.

JOY. Grandma can I get your clothes for you?

EARLY. I'll change after I eat.

> (**JOY** *pulls out a chair for* **EARLY**.)

Don't be pullin' out my chair.

I'm too tired to get up just yet.

JOY. But it's breakfast, Grandma.

EARLY. Think I'll have my meals right here from now on.

It's such a comfortable chair.

> (**HA-HA** *enters, dressed in day clothes, drying his face with a towel, and walks to the table.*)

HA-HA. ...

Um. Mom?

JOY. Oh, right.

> (**JOY** *lets* **HA-HA** *take her place beside* **GAIL**.)

GAIL. ...

JOY. I told him we could switch.

GAIL. ...

EARLY. Who sayin' the good morning prayer?

Okay I will.

...

Dear God, these some messed up sinners over here. Gathered around the table like some hogs. They don't give a damn about you. Just leanin' over they food like heifers over a trough. But your mercy is great, God. And your bounty overfloweth. Thank you for all the seasons. And thank you for the angels. And thank you for letting us survive as long as we have out here. And may you continue to bless us Lord and also may certain ones among us start fathering some babies so our little clan don't die out forever.

And speaking of dying: may those of us who are about to do that not waste our final, precious hours. Amen.

JOY. Amen.

HA-HA. Amen.

GAIL. Ha-Ha, bring great grandma her plate.

(**HA-HA** *brings* **EARLY** *her plate.*)

(*Everyone begins to eat.*)

EARLY. Thank you, sweetie.

You know: making a baby is not much harder than bringing someone a plate.

JOY. Grandma, he's not ready for that yet –

GAIL. Grandma Early, I was gonna take the truck into town today to get looked at –

EARLY. Don't try to change the subject on me –

GAIL. I'm sayin' I can take him with me and we can stop by the library. There's a group of young ladies that hang out there after school and they like him. All the girls like him –

HA-HA. They don't *like* me, we just use the computers across from / each other. –

GAIL. False modesty does not become us, Ha-Ha.

I could barely tear you away from their graspy little hands last time –

HA-HA. But it ain't *like* that –

EARLY. Good then, that's good.

GAIL. I think it's time for you to start drivin'! What you think Ha-Ha?

HA-HA. I can drive the truck?

GAIL. Sure. On the way back. After the mechanic takes a look at the gears.

I'll drive into town and you'll drive back.

HA-HA. Cool –

GAIL. And this week you can study for the driving test and once you have a license you can take yourself to the library. Whenever you want to read a new book. Or if you want some company your own age –

EARLY. Yes, alright –

JOY. Maybe not every day –

GAIL. Anytime he feels the need –

JOY. We can't afford the gas.

GAIL. It's not *that* far –

JOY. Still –

GAIL. Don't *still* me.

JOY. ...

I was thinkin' about goin' in and looking for work myself.

GAIL. What you gonna do?

JOY. I don't know. Waitressing. Sign holding. Whatever I can get.

GAIL. Don't want you doin' none of that, baby. I got it covered.

HA-HA. But you're gonna be dead.

GAIL. I WILL DIE WHEN I'M GOOD AND READY!

...

...

(To **HA-HA**.*)* Go sit over there.

(**HA-HA** *moves to an empty chair.*)

(They all eat in silence...)

JOY. Was actually thinking come spring I could take up Daddy's old job.

EARLY. You gonna take Walking Man's old job?

GAIL. No, baby –

EARLY. That's a man's job. That should be Ha-Ha's job –

JOY. NO!

GAIL. I don't know about that, Grandma Early –

JOY. So help me God –

HA-HA. Grandpa's job? Helping farmers?

I could help farmers –

GAIL. Ha-Ha, that was Walking Man's thing and he did it well. But don't nobody needs to follow in his footsteps.

That is not what this household is about.

We ain't come out here to have y'all follow in no footsteps.

We here so y'all can have the…the *perspective* you need –

EARLY. Yes –

GAIL. To figure out your own footsteps –

EARLY. Yes that's right –

GAIL. And you will.

We'll get by.

We always have and we always will.

EARLY. Look at Gail. Figuring things out. It's never too late to learn.

(A silence. Everyone finishes their food.)

JOY. Y'all can leave your dishes, I'll get 'em.

HA-HA. Thanks, mama.

*(**HA-HA** retrieves his book.)*

GAIL. Put that book away, we gotta go.

*(**GAIL** goes to the coat rack and puts on her jacket.)*

HA-HA. We goin' now?

GAIL. Yes, what you think?

HA-HA. Just me and you?

GAIL. Where do your mind be, child?!

*(**GAIL** exits. **HA-HA** grabs his jacket and hurries after her.)*

JOY. Want me to bring you your clothes, grandma?

EARLY. Oh no, is you mad at me, too?

JOY. Why are you being so mean to Mom?

EARLY. ...

Mom?

JOY. Gail.

...

Grandma. I'm saying you need to be nice to Gail.

EARLY. Gail ain't nobody.

JOY. She takes good care of you.

EARLY. *You* take good care of me.

You don't act like I'm a burden.

JOY. ...

EARLY. ...

How come you don't sing no more?

JOY. Sing?

EARLY. You used to sing all the time.

JOY. Sing what?

EARLY. Used to sing about whatever you was doing. Used to skip around the house and dance around the house singing about the walls, the chairs, the door – didn't matter.

How come you don't do that no more?

JOY. ...

I'm older now, Grandma.

EARLY. So what, you still *you* ain't you?

JOY. ...

EARLY. Go ahead.

JOY. ...

EARLY. Go ahead and sing.

JOY. Not with you watching me like that.

EARLY. What you can't sing for your old grandma?

Okay, never mind.

...

(**JOY** *gets a spray bottle from the cupboard, sprays the table and wipes it down with a cloth.*)

(*She begins to sing.*)

JOY.
GONNA WASH THE TABLE TABLE CLEAN, CLEEEEEAN, SO CLEEEEEEAN,

EARLY. Alright!

JOY.
GONNA MAKE IT SPARKLE LIKE THE SPRIIIIIIING.

EARLY. Yes you are!

JOY.
THAT'S WHAT HAPPENS WHEN I DO MY THIIIIIING!

EARLY. Alright, show 'em what happens!

JOY.
OH YEAH, I DOOOOO MYYYY, THIIIIING!

EARLY. There you go, Joy! There you go!

JOY.
CAN'T BELIEVE MY BABY GONNA DRIIIIVE TODAY!

EARLY. Believe it!

JOY.
I HOPE I HOPE HE DOESN'T CRASH, I PRAY!

EARLY. Protect him, Lord, protect him!

JOY.
GONNA FIND A GIRLFRIEND AT THE LIBRARAAAAAY!

EARLY. Yes! Yes! Where he gonna find her?

JOY.
THE LIBRARAAAAAY!

EARLY. You're so talented, Joy.

JOY. …

EARLY. I'm glad when you left, you ain't leave us for good.

JOY. …

Gonna go wash these dishes.

>   (**JOY** *exits.*)

>   (**EARLY** *goes into the bedroom.*

>   *She opens a dresser drawer and pulls out a tobacco pipe.*)

>   (*She lights it and smokes.*)

EARLY. What?

Lookin' at me like *what's she doin' here.*

This is *my* room.

And it's my pipe.

Found it under some brush right by that tree there. Saw the stem sticking out.

Plucked it like a rose.

Yes, this pipe knows who saved it from the moss.

Walking Man decided to start smokin' it every day. Fine. Fine by me.

And then, you know, a cow fell on him.

And now Gail think she has the right to it.

…

What the hell kinda way is that to die?

…

My husband. Edward. Ha! He ain't know how to die right either. Had every opportunity to. Got both his legs shot up in the war. First one got shot, and he just kept hoppin' at the Nazis. So they shot his other leg.

We always used to ask Crazy Eddie – that's what he wanted us to call him after he got back, "Crazy Eddie" – we'd say, "Crazy Eddie, why ain't you just lay down after they got your *first* leg?"

And he'd smile from here all the way back to Tennessee and he'd say:

"It was World War *Two*.

One leg wouldn't do."

...

He refused to let the doctors operate on him. Said his bullets was *gaining interest*.

He refused to stop driving, too.

You can imagine how that ended.

...

We had to put a new engine in his truck. And a new windshield.

And now Gail trying to kill that thing again, drivin' it all over the whole godforsaken county.

But that's Gail for you. Messin' everything up.

Bless her heart,

There's some people in life, no matter how good they try to be, you just ain't never gonna like 'em. You've decided.

I decided about Gail when she brought that lighter into the house.

I allowed it to stay, just like I allowed her to stay.

For Walking Man's sake.

EARLY. But I ain't never laid a finger on it. 'Cause I know where it really came from. And I know *who* it really came from.

And that's a long, long story that I ain't gonna start right now.

...

Me and Edward we built this place together. Scrap by scrap. Put us up a little canopy right out there. Slept in it. Did the thing in it, you know. While we wasn't workin' on the house.

I shouldn't lie to you and make it sound like the movies. It wasn't. Well, it was a little bit. He loved me like the movies. But I was with him just…well, just to get away, really. Took a while for the love to set in on my end.

...

He would kiss me with his whole mouth and I'd let it in. Let it in and just keep on breathin'. And that was okay. That was fine. He coulda been anybody, really. But he was Ed. Edward. Crazy Eddie.

And I was Early. And I still am.

I still am.

    (**EARLY** *smokes the pipe.*)

Two

(Night.)

(In the main room, all are asleep in the same places as the night before: **JOY** *on the sofa bed,* **EARLY** *in her chair,* **HA-HA** *on the floor.)*

(In the bedroom, **GAIL** *is sitting up in her bed.)*

(She is actively not looking at **WALKING MAN**, *who bangs on the window.)*

WALKING MAN. Gail.

...

Abigail.

> *(***WALKING MAN** *rattles the window until it opens.)*

WALKING MAN. Gail, talk to me for a minute –

GAIL. Don't even think about tryna climb through there –

WALKING MAN. If I wanna come in, I'll come in through the *door* –

GAIL. *Then close my window, then –*

WALKING MAN. Ain't climbin' through no window –

GAIL. *Close my window, then –*

WALKING MAN. *Your* window. Please, I built / this window –

GAIL. You did not build this window, Walking Man –

WALKING MAN. How you gonna tell me I didn't build the window when I built the window –

GAIL. Your daddy and your mama / built that window,

WALKING MAN. No they did not build this window –

GAIL. Just like they built these walls, just like they built the roof, just like they laid down / the floor, just like they built the outhouse –

WALKING MAN. Right, and as soon as I came back here –

Soon as I came back here to help out my mama –

GAIL. Do not talk to me about that woman –

WALKING MAN. First thing my mama / asked me to do was install a new window –

GAIL. Do not talk to me about that woman. She's being terrible to me –

WALKING MAN. I installed this window. And you know I installed this window, and I know you know I installed it 'cause how many times you asked me, why couldn't I put a bigger window in –

GAIL. I like to have some light –

WALKING MAN. Like I'm supposed to know what specifications you wanted –

GAIL. I don't give a damn about the specifications I just like to have light in my room –

WALKING MAN. With your Home and Garden TV watchin' ass –

GAIL. Where's a TV, we ain't got no TV –

WALKING MAN. At Christmas / you be watchin' TV –

GAIL. The one time a year when we visit *my folks* and I'm near a TV damn right I watch a TV. You *shoulda* put in some electric. *Window* Man.

WALKING MAN. ...

That's it, I'm comin' in.

GAIL. Don't I'm 'sleep.

*(**WALKING MAN** walks around the house to the door.)*

WALKING MAN DON'T COME UP IN HERE HAUNTING MY HOUSE!

WALKING MAN. SHOULDA TALKED TO ME, THEN!

GAIL. I WAS TALKING TO YOU!

*(**WALKING MAN** comes in through the front door.)*

JOY. *(Waking up.)* Daddy?

WALKING MAN. Go to sleep baby girl I'm just gonna have a little talk with your mama.

JOY. Love you.

WALKING MAN. Love you, sweetness.

HA-HA. Hey grandpa.

WALKING MAN. Go back to sleep, little man.

HA-HA. Okay.

*(**WALKING MAN** knocks on the door to the bedroom.)*

WALKING MAN. May I come in, please?

GAIL. …

Don't touch the bed.

*(**WALKING MAN** enters the bedroom.)*

WALKING MAN. Why I can't touch the bed?

GAIL. Don't want you breathin' all up on it with your dead man breath.

WALKING MAN. Not my fault I ain't alive.

GAIL. …

WALKING MAN. You can't hear me out?

GAIL. What you want?

WALKING MAN. ...

Hi, Gail.

GAIL. Hello.

WALKING MAN. We ain't talked.

GAIL. ...

WALKING MAN. You don't have to be mad at me.

GAIL. ...

How'd you let the cow fall on you? How'd you let that happen?

WALKING MAN. ...

I was just doin' my thing like I always do, you know.

Went out and did my rounds at the farms.

It was almost sunset. It was my last slaughter of the day.

And this particular heifer she was...I don't know.

She was kinda lookin' at me.

Like, we made eye contact.

And I'm thinkin', why are me and this cow havin' this moment?

I'm just here to kill it real quick, now we havin' a moment, now it's some weirdly intimate energy goin' on between me and this cow, so I don't feel like I can just shoot it.

But I've already been paid for the job, see? So I can't *not* kill it.

And I start thinkin': this cow:

What she needs, what she's askin' for,

Is a real death.

Old school, you see what I'm sayin'?

So I take out my knife.

GAIL. You don't carry a knife.

WALKING MAN. I do carry a knife. My gray knife.

GAIL. That's a *switchblade*.

WALKING MAN. That's a knife.

GAIL. You can't kill no cow with that.

WALKING MAN. Yeah, well, that's where things started to go off track.

GAIL. ...

WALKING MAN. So I walk up to her and I put my hand on her shoulder. And she steps on my foot.

Hurts like hell, but I'm thinkin' she's probably just tryna return the gesture. 'Cause she don't have no hands. So you know, that's the best she can do, so I accept it.

And I say to her, "Thank you. Thank you for feedin' this family you about to feed. And thank you for helping me to feed me and my family." And I take a breath. And I plunge that blade into her jugular.

And she screams like you wouldn't believe. And takes off running. But my knife is handle deep, and my fist is kinda lodged up in there, so I'm startin' to get dragged around, so I kinda heave myself on top of her, and blood is sprayin' every which way, and now I'm feeling like: maybe I made the wrong choice. But it's too late to change course now. All I can think to do is keep on stabbin'.

So I'm goin' for it. Hard as I can. And I feel my arms turning to rubber. And then I can't feel my arms at all. And finally. Finally, she tips over. Rolls right on top of me. Rolls up on my stomach. My ribs don't just crack, they *snap*. Like celery stalks. And I'm losin' air quick,

I know I got but maybe one scream in me – and don't think I didn't scream, now. I screamed with some *purpose*.

But these folks on this farm...

You know how it is with these new school farmers. They had left my payment in an envelope on the porch – probably went up to the city for the day. So they wouldn't have to be nowhere near it. Hopin' they'd come home and she'd be all chopped up, wrapped up and put away. But instead,

There we were.

...

You know when things go wrong like that it's never just one thing. It's a lot of things goin' just the right kinda wrong all at once.

GAIL. ...

Ha-Ha found some book at the library today.

Said he wants to be a vegan now.

WALKING MAN. Good.

GAIL. If he gonna be a vegan we all gonna have to do it. Can't be making separate meals for everybody.

WALKING MAN. That's good, then,

GAIL. What am I gonna cook?

WALKING MAN. ...

Gail –

GAIL. I been hearing you knockin' on my door.

Every night.

WALKING MAN. I know. I know you hear me.

GAIL. I don't want to.

I don't want to hear you.

WALKING MAN. I know you don't.

GAIL. Then why are you making me hear you?

WALKING MAN. It hurt me to die, Gail.

> The bones breakin', the breath leavin', I could handle that. But baby, the real weight:
>
> The real weight was thinkin' about you. And Joy and Ha-Ha. And Mom.
>
> Knowing what I couldn't do for y'all no more.
>
> It's a crazy world you live in.
>
> One split second and allasudden, I couldn't do a single thing for ya.
>
> Couldn't even spare you the anxiousness of wonderin' where I was.
>
> Or the shock when you heard the news.
>
> Couldn't do just one more deed for the ones I love.
>
> And that was hell. Those seconds were eternities of hell. Each one of 'em.
>
> I don't want that for you.

GAIL. But that's exactly what you're putting me through! Comin' up in here tellin' everyone I'm about to die, now that's all I'm thinkin' about. All the things I won't be able to do for the family.

WALKING MAN. I didn't know you'd take it that way.

GAIL. How was I supposed to take it?

WALKING MAN. By doin' what you do. What you always do.

> By getting things in order.

GAIL. ...

WALKING MAN. So you prepared to let go when the time comes.

GAIL. ...

WALKING MAN. It's all gonna be okay.

GAIL. ...

WALKING MAN. You don't have to hold up these walls no more /

My mama gonna be alright –

GAIL. Then who's going to –

WALKING MAN. Joy gonna be alright –

GAIL. Who's holdin 'em up, Walking Man?

WALKING MAN. Our grandson gonna be alright –

GAIL. This house ain't keepin itself straight, not past winter. Gonna have to put some money into it.

WALKING MAN. I'm tellin' you, you don't need to worry 'bout any of that anymore –

GAIL. Stop tellin' me that –

WALKING MAN. It's the truth –

GAIL. The truth needs to learn when to keep its mouth shut.

WALKING MAN. Alright.

>   (**WALKING MAN** *sits on a chair by the dresser.* **GAIL** *sits on the bed.*)
>
>   (*They look at each other.*)
>
>   (*They look.*)
>
>   (*They look.*)

GAIL. Joy wants to take up your old job come spring.

WALKING MAN. I wouldn't recommend it.

GAIL. Great Grandma thinks Ha-Ha should do it.

WALKING MAN. Our grandson, Ha-Ha.

GAIL. Mhmm.

WALKING MAN. The vegan.

GAIL. Mhmm.

WALKING MAN. Slaughtering farm animals?

GAIL. Yes.

WALKING MAN. Okay.

GAIL. Your mother says it's a man's job.

WALKING MAN. Okay.

GAIL. I think Ha-Ha should do it. It would be hard for him. But it would be good for him.

WALKING MAN. Boy has a hard enough time cuttin' the grass.

GAIL. Well he's gotta learn the ways of the world sometime.

WALKING MAN. Why?

GAIL. ...What do you mean, why?

WALKING MAN. What's so great about the world?

Let him do what he do.

GAIL. He reads.

WALKING MAN. Let him work in a bookstore or somethin'.

Let him follow his interests.

GAIL. We'd have to move.

We'd have to leave the house.

WALKING MAN. That's alright.

GAIL. It is not. Alright. With me.

WALKING MAN. ...

GAIL. All I ever had I gave to this house.

All my dreams I poured into these dreams.

And you want to come back here, like God's Happy Angel,

And tell me that it's all...nothing.

That it's all unimportant.

WALKING MAN. ...

That's right.

GAIL. ...

...

When you reckon I'm gonna die?

WALKING MAN. Tomorrow night.

GAIL. Tomorrow night.

WALKING MAN. Yes.

GAIL. How you reckon I'm gonna die?

WALKING MAN. You gonna crash my father's truck.

GAIL. ...

What if I don't drive the truck?

WALKING MAN. ...

GAIL. Will I die some other way?

WALKING MAN. ...

GAIL. Walking Man.

WALKING MAN. Your questions are very. Uh...

GAIL. What?

WALKING MAN. They're not *bad* questions.

GAIL. ...Okay.

WALKING MAN. It's kind of like you...like when Joy was little. And whenever we'd take her into town to get her shots –

GAIL. Oh, Joy and her shots!

WALKING MAN. Sounded like she was gettin axe murdered, right?

GAIL. As soon as the doctor would touch her,

AH! AH! AH! What are you doing!? WHAT ARE YOU DOING TO ME!?

WALKING MAN. Yeah.

Like that.

GAIL. ...

What?

WALKING MAN. It's logical questions.

"What are you doing to me?"

"Is it going to hurt?"

"When am I going to die?"

"How am I going to die?"

Logical questions. But also kind of, you know,

Worldly questions.

GAIL. Well, I guess that's 'cause I'm trying to stay in the world, Walking Man.

WALKING MAN. For Joy it was all about the treat.

Holdin' her head up so she couldn't see the needle. "What kind of treat do you want when it's over? Cake or ice cream? What flavor? Rocky road? Good choice, rocky road is good. What's your favorite part of rocky road? The marshmallows? Me too. I never see 'em comin'."

WALKING MAN. And then, little Joy, she knew. That there was somethin' on the other side of the pain. And she was alright.

So: what's yours?

GAIL. ...

WALKING MAN. What you need, Gail?

GAIL. ...

WALKING MAN. Just say it.

Ain't no shame, just say it.

GAIL. ...

I want Grandma Early to be happy.

WALKING MAN. And what do you think would make her happy?

GAIL. A baby. A baby in the family.

WALKING MAN. ...

GAIL. Even if Ha-Ha had a girlfriend, you know. If he…if he was kind of on the path. That would be somethin'.

WALKING MAN. Yeah…

GAIL. He's not ready yet.

I took him out to the library today and there was a whole gang of girls smilin' at him and he just…I don't know. He's a good boy.

WALKING MAN. How he s'pose to meet girls hangin' out with his grandmother at the library?

GAIL. ...

Probably just as well.

We shouldn't be rushing him.

...

WALKING MAN. I'll talk to him.

GAIL. You will?

WALKING MAN. I will.

GAIL. Thank you.

WALKING MAN. ...

You gonna go to sleep now?

GAIL. ...

What's it like?

What's it like over there?

WALKING MAN. Peaceful.

GAIL. How peaceful?

WALKING MAN. So peaceful, peace don't know nothin' about it.

GAIL. Is there food?

WALKING MAN. Yeah.

GAIL. You lyin'.

WALKING MAN. No, there's you know, banquets.

GAIL. What other lies you wanna tell me?

WALKING MAN. When have I ever lied to you?

GAIL. I don't know. You have, though.

WALKING MAN. There's songs.

GAIL. Songs?

WALKING MAN. Gail, there's songs.

Songs like the songs you know.

But you know them even better. You know all their secrets.

GAIL. Will I be able to learn the violin?

WALKING MAN. Any instrument you want.

GAIL. I want the violin.

WALKING MAN. But over here you won't only play it.

You'll become its voice.

It's real over here.

Everything is real.

GAIL. ...

And peaceful, you said?

WALKING MAN. Yes.

GAIL. ...

Peace is real?

WALKING MAN. Peace is real.

GAIL. ...

...

What time is it?

WALKING MAN. I'll talk to Ha-Ha.

GAIL. ...

Thank you.

...

What time is it?

WALKING MAN. Late.

Early.

GAIL. ...

How late?

...

How early?

WALKING MAN. ...

> (**GAIL** *is asleep.*)
>
> (**WALKING MAN** *opens a dresser drawer.*)
>
> (*He pulls out a set of clothes.*)
>
> (*He goes into the main room.*)
>
> (*He jostles* **HA-HA** *awake.*)

HA-HA. Hey, Grandpa.

WALKING MAN. *(Handing him the clothes.)* How well can you drive?

HA-HA. Drove back from the library today.

Grandma was in the car with me.

WALKING MAN. You know how to get to Carbondale?

HA-HA. Uhhh...

WALKING MAN. You go out to the highway and follow the signs that say "Carbondale."

HA-HA. Okay.

WALKING MAN. You need to go to Carbondale.

HA-HA. Right now?

WALKING MAN. You wanna be back in time for dinner, don't you?

HA-HA. Yes.

WALKING MAN. Alright. So go on over to Carbondale. And when you get there...

> (**WALKING MAN** *reaches deep – almost impossibly deep – into his pocket. He pulls out a wad of bills.*)

WALKING MAN. *(Handing the wad of bills to* **HA-HA.***)* When you get there, you, uh…

Ha-Ha, you need to make a friend.

HA-HA. …

WALKING MAN. A woman friend.

HA-HA. Okay.

WALKING MAN. Not a *woman* woman. Not too old. A girlfriend.

HA-HA. Okay.

WALKING MAN. Not a little girl. Not like a kid. A teenager.

HA-HA. …

WALKING MAN. But not…not a thirteen-year-old.

HA-HA. An older teenager. Someone my age.

WALKING MAN. Yes. Exactly. You get it.

HA-HA. Okay.

WALKING MAN. That's what the money's for.

HA-HA. …

WALKING MAN. Because often times, people have a hard time.

HA-HA. …

WALKING MAN. It's not always easy to make a friend. So you can, uh. You can pay a woman. And she'll show you how to make friends.

And then you'll know. What it's like to have a friend. And then you'll want to have a friend all the time. That's…how it works. Okay?

HA-HA. …

Yes.

WALKING MAN. Do you know what I'm talking about, Ha-Ha?

HA-HA. Yeah.

WALKING MAN. ...

I'm saying you need to buy some pussy, Ha-Ha.

HA-HA. Okay.

WALKING MAN. Not a cat. Don't come home with a cat.

HA-HA. I won't.

WALKING MAN. Hurry up. Drive slow. But not too slow.

Be back before sundown or you'll worry everybody.

> (**HA-HA** *grabs his jacket and exits.*)

Sweet dreams, Joy.

JOY. *(Not really awake.)* Okay...

> (**EARLY** *opens her eyes and looks at* **WALKING MAN.**)

WALKING MAN. ...

EARLY. Say hi to the river for me.

WALKING MAN. Yes, ma'am.

> (**WALKING MAN** *exits.*)

Three

(Afternoon.)

*(**EARLY** is hanging clothes on a line outside. Perhaps she can be seen outside the house and/or through the window.)*

*(**GAIL** is organizing the bookshelf.)*

*(**JOY** is palpably anxious.)*

GAIL. Don't be anxious. He'll be back. He'll be fine.

JOY. ...

How many times you gonna rearrange those books?

GAIL. Only once if I can get it right.

JOY. You been at it all morning, all afternoon, when you gonna finish?

GAIL. I'll finish when I finish stop looking over my shoulder.

JOY. I'm gonna go help Great Grandma hang that laundry.

GAIL. Leave her be. The sun's out. Ain't gonna be many more days like this before winter, let her enjoy herself.

JOY. Well I need *something* to do besides worry.

GAIL. ...

*(**JOY** watches her grandmother through the window.)*

JOY. Why she so good at that?

The clothes just drape so *right* when she drapes 'em.

GAIL. Practice.

JOY. I practice. They don't drape like that for me.

GAIL. Uhuh. That's why.

JOY. What's why?

GAIL. *They don't drape like that for me.*

'Cause you entitled.

JOY. You raised me.

GAIL. I ain't raise you.

JOY. …

GAIL. I facilitated your growth.

JOY. Oh.

GAIL. *Tried* to raise you. But you wasn't havin' none of that.

No ma'am. Not my Joy. My precious, impossible, anxious little Joy.

*(**JOY** paces around…)*

JOY. How good of a driver is he? Scale of one to ten.

GAIL. I'd say about a one.

JOY. Oh my God, Mother.

GAIL. He's got the truck, he'll be fine.

JOY. How can you be sure?

GAIL. …

Because I talked to your father last night.

JOY. You did?

GAIL. I did. Nice, long talk.

JOY. …Okay.

GAIL. Thought I'd hear him out.

JOY. …

GAIL. Turns out I'm s'pose to die *tonight*.

JOY. ...

GAIL. *In* the truck.

JOY. ...

Oh.

GAIL. So there you go.

JOY. ...

GAIL. Ha-Ha has the truck, he left in the truck. He's coming back as sure as I'm leaving out.

JOY. ...

You're sure Daddy said you / would be –

GAIL. I said, *How you reckon I'm gonna die?*

He said, *You gonna crash my father's truck.*

JOY. ...

Mom?

GAIL. Yes, Joy?

JOY. I don't want you to die.

GAIL. Like you said, I'll come by at night.

JOY. That's not the same at all.

GAIL. Well it's not supposed to be the same, is it?

JOY. The house is gonna fall apart without you.

GAIL. Joy. I'm trying not to think that way and you pushing me right back into it.

JOY. It's true.

GAIL. When Grandma Early came out here for the first time she wasn't much older than Ha-Ha is now. Can you believe that?

And she was here all by herself. She found her way, just like you'll find yours.

JOY. I thought Grandma and Crazy Eddie built the house *together*.

GAIL. Yes, they did.

…

Eventually.

But before that, and before the house, it was just her.

JOY. I never knew that.

GAIL. …

Grandma Early loves you so much. You can't do no wrong in her eyes.

JOY. …

GAIL. You might not know it, Joy, but you've held us all together. You've been doing it your whole life. You always come through.

Even when it seems like you won't. Hindsight is 20/20 of course, but when you ran off to Springfield to become a pole dancer –

JOY. Mama –

GAIL. I know you don't like talkin' about it –

JOY. I didn't "run off to become a pole dancer" –

GAIL. I'm just saying that had I known –

JOY. I needed to make my way in the world for a while –

GAIL. I know you did –

JOY. I needed to do my own kind of growin' up –

GAIL. And what I'm sayin' –

JOY. I barely even used the pole I was never any good at the pole.

GAIL. ...

Even so.

Had I known you were gonna disappear out of our lives like that and then one day just show up at the door. With that precious baby...

Show up sayin', "Mama, can we stay?"

...

Mama can we stay.

...I'd say it was music to my ears but I ain't never heard music that sweet.

...

Those were some dark days for us when you were gone.

And then you came back with our most prized gift of all.

And that was a sign.

Walking Man and I took that as a sign. That we had done right.

That little baby. That little generation breathing life back into all of us.

...

It's not really fair to Ha-Ha, is it?

All our expectations on his skinny shoulders.

...

Just love that boy.

You gotta do your work and you gotta love that boy.

And he will bring you gifts you never knew were comin'.

(**EARLY** *enters with a dead squirrel.*)

EARLY. Clubbed me a squirrel!

JOY. Nononono, Grandma –

>   (**EARLY** *plops the squirrel onto the table.*)

EARLY. Gail, get over here and skin it.

GAIL. Grandma, we can't leave it on the counter.

EARLY. What have you done today, Gail?

GAIL. Not quite as much as you, Grandma.

EARLY. You damn right.

GAIL. Do you want to tell us what you've done, Grandma Early?

EARLY. Got up at sunrise. Washed myself. Washed the clothes. Washed every piece of fabric in this house, matterafact. Hung it all out to dry. Went down to the river for water. For that good water. *My* water.

Picked up Walking Man from the library and sat with him and did his math with him. He's good at math except he's too impatient. Wants to do all the steps at once. Wants to skip steps. I told him you can skip steps once you know the steps. Once they in your blood. That's when you can skip 'em. 'Cause you ain't really skippin 'em then, is you? You just takin' the escalator.

GAIL. ...

We gonna have to put the squirrel back outside, Grandma Early.

EARLY. How come you being so nice?

JOY. Gail is always nice to you, Grandma.

EARLY. Yes, but usually she angry underneath.

How come you ain't angry no more?

GAIL. We just need to put the squirrel outside, alright?

EARLY. You hear that? No anger!

Just 'cause you ain't angry at me don't think I can't be angry at you.

GAIL. That's fine.

EARLY. I'll be angry at you if I want to and there ain't nothin' you can do about it. The damage has been done.

GAIL. Let's just let the squirrel out.

EARLY. Why?

GAIL. Ha-Ha's gonna be coming home soon and he doesn't eat meat.

EARLY. He don't?

GAIL. Not anymore, no.

EARLY. Why didn't you tell me that, then! That's good meat. That's good meat and it's gonna rot. It's gonna rot because of you. Just like everything else around here.

(Banging on the table.)

Rotting! Rotting! Rotting! Rotting! Rotting!

Whose fault is that!?

GAIL. Do you want to tell us whose fault it is?

EARLY. No, you!

You say it.

You own up to it.

GAIL. ...

It's my fault.

EARLY. Say it one more time. One more time. Say it slower.

GAIL. It's –

EARLY. Nah-ah. No. Look me in the eye.

And say it slow.

GAIL. It's.

My.

Fault.

EARLY. ...

...

Why did you do it?

GAIL. ...

EARLY. Why did you let me just walk out into wilderness? Why'd you just let me go like I was nothin'?

...

Like I was a rock?

...

Like I was mud?

GAIL. ...

EARLY. Well, I built a house.

Did you know that?

GAIL. ...

EARLY. I took all that nothin' you gave me. And I built a house.

And it's still standin'. It's standin'.

And I dare you to knock it down.

Knock it down and watch what I do.

Knock it down and watch me build it again.

And again.

And again.

And again.

(**EARLY** *sits in her chair.*)

JOY. ...

...

...

Grandma Early, would you like some tea?

EARLY. No thank you, sugar.

JOY. Want a book to read?

EARLY. Think I'll take a rest.

JOY. I'll get you a blanket.

(**JOY** *gets a blanket for* **EARLY**.)

(**EARLY** *stares off into space.*)

GAIL. ...

JOY. ...

(**GAIL** *throws the squirrel out the door.*)

(**JOY** *stands still.*)

(**GAIL** *stands still.*)

(*They stand.*)

(*They stand.*)

Are you gonna stay for dinner at least?

GAIL. I don't know about that, baby.

(**GAIL** *returns to the bookshelf and resumes her task of rearranging the books.*)

(*The front door cracks open.*)

(**HA-HA** *peaks his head in.*)

JOY. Ha-Ha!

HA-HA. Hi Mama. Hi, Grandma Gail.

GAIL. What you doin standin' out there?

HA-HA. I made a friend.

JOY. ...

HA-HA. Can she come in, too?

GAIL. ...

JOY. ...

Of course, baby.

>*(**HA-HA** comes all the way in.)*

>*(Behind him enters **SYMPHONY**. She is enthralled at the surroundings.)*

HA-HA. ...

SYMPHONY. Hello.

I'm Symphony.

JOY. Hi, I'm Joy. I'm Ha-Ha's mother.

Ha-Ha, you s'pose to introduce people.

HA-HA. Symphony, this is my mother. Her name is Joy.

SYMPHONY. Hi!

HA-HA. And this is Great Grandma Early.

SYMPHONY. Hi, so nice to meet you.

>*(**EARLY** stares off into space.)*

HA-HA. Great Grandma, this is my new friend.

Her name is Symphony.

>*(**EARLY** stares off into space.)*

JOY. Grandma Early is a little tired.

She hung all that laundry on the line, did you see it?

SYMPHONY. Oh, yes, I did!

JOY. This is my mother, Ha-Ha's grandmother, Gail.

Ha-Ha, will you get some tea for Great Grandma?

HA-HA. Yes, ma'am.

> (**HA-HA** *pours water into the kettle and places it on the stove.*)

GAIL. Symphony, where are you from?

SYMPHONY. Everywhere.

But Carbondale.

But more like everywhere.

JOY. You go to SIU?

SYMPHONY. Not at the moment, no. Just, you know,

In Carbondale.

HA-HA. I don't know if I want to go to college either.

SYMPHONY. You should! You'd love college.

HA-HA. Do they let you read what you want to?

SYMPHONY. I mean, maybe. If you make a case for it.

HA-HA. ...

Do you like books?

SYMPHONY. Yeah.

HA-HA. We have a bookshelf.

> (**HA-HA** *and* **SYMPHONY** *go to the bookshelf. They stand by it, looking at the titles.* **GAIL** *and* **JOY** *sit down and watch them.*)

SYMPHONY. Cool.

(**HA-HA** *takes a book off of the shelf.*)

HA-HA. Are you gonna pick one?

SYMPHONY. We're gonna stand here and *read*?

Like, now?

HA-HA. Yeah.

Unless you don't want to.

SYMPHONY. I mean I like reading, but like...

What else do you do?

HA-HA. Um...think.

Cook.

Plant.

Fix stuff.

Wash clothes.

Walk.

SYMPHONY. You forgot *drive to Carbondale and pick up chicks.*

HA-HA. Oh.

Yeah.

SYMPHONY. ...

Do you ever, like,

Laugh?

HA-HA. Sometimes, yeah.

SYMPHONY. Is Ha-Ha your real name?

HA-HA. Yes.

SYMPHONY. 'Cause you sort of take yourself really seriously.

For someone named Ha-Ha.

So...No offense.

...

HA-HA. None taken.

SYMPHONY. That was supposed to make you laugh.

>   (**HA-HA** *tries to laugh.*)

Oh my God, that laugh is so fake.

>   (**HA-HA** *keeps trying.*)

Ew, stop it!

>   (**HA-HA** *stops.*)

Well, your smile is real at least.

...

>   (**SYMPHONY** *lunges at* **HA-HA** *and playfully grabs him around the waist.*)
>
>   (**HA-HA** *is extremely ticklish and laughs/ screams/freaks out. It's a little more of a reaction than she had bargained for.*)

HA-HA. I gotta get Great Grandma her tea.

>   (**EARLY** *has been looking at* **SYMPHONY** *and* **HA-HA** *for some time now...*)

EARLY. (*To* **SYMPHONY**.) Hello.

SYMPHONY. Hi.

EARLY. Glad you made it.

SYMPHONY. I'm Symphony.

EARLY. Yes, you are.

HA-HA. Here's your tea, Great Grandma.

EARLY. I don't need no tea.

HA-HA. Okay.

> (**EARLY** *rises from her chair and walks to* **SYMPHONY**.)

EARLY. ...

Hm.

Alright.

SYMPHONY. ...

EARLY. How'd you get your name, Symphony?

SYMPHONY. Oh, I was just kinda born with it, no big deal.

EARLY. You don't know who named you?

SYMPHONY. Oh! It was my grandmother's choice. She passed on before I was born. But, yeah. She got in the name request!

EARLY. ...

You got you a heart.

You got you a soul.

SYMPHONY. ...

Thank you.

> (**EARLY** *sits back down in her chair.*)

SYMPHONY. *(To* **HA-HA** *re: the books.)* Do you have any recommendations?

HA-HA. ...Oh!

This one.

> (**HA-HA** *gives* **SYMPHONY** *a book.*)

>   (**HA-HA** and **SYMPHONY** *stand and read.*)

GAIL. …

Well, then.

>   (**GAIL** *picks up the car key and puts on her coat.*)

JOY. Mama, you're leaving right now?

GAIL. Yes I am.

JOY. …

Mama?

GAIL. Yes?

JOY. You don't have to get in the truck. You don't have to drive anywhere until you're ready.

GAIL. …

…

Today's the first day in my life I've felt old.

First day in my life.

It feels nice to be serene for a change.

Feels nice to slow down and know you couldn't speed up even if you wanted to.

JOY. …

What should I cook?

What should I make for dinner?

GAIL. We got some squash, I think. We got some onions. You'll figure it out.

JOY. How many eggs we got left?

Do we have enough for breakfast?

Should I save some to bake with?

How many eggs should I set aside to bake with?

HA-HA. Mama, I don't eat eggs.

JOY. YES YOU DO.

HA-HA. No, I don't.

JOY. YOU GONNA EAT WHAT I PUT ON THE TABLE. END OF STORY.

HA-HA. I'm a vegan.

JOY. You can eat what I put on the table, or you can drive yourself back to the library, get that vegetable book off the shelf and bring it here so I can slap you with it.

Sorry, Symphony.

HA-HA. It's not a *vegetable book*.

JOY. …

HA-HA. It's called *Healthy Planet, Healthy People*.

It's really good, you should read it.

JOY. Did you just talk back to me?

HA-HA. …

JOY. Mama, Ha-Ha talked back to me.

He got fresh.

He brought a girl home and now he's getting fresh WHAT DO I DO?!

GAIL. He's seventeen. It's normal.

It's fine.

JOY. It's not fine, Mama.

I'M NOT FINE!

(**GAIL** *starts to laugh.*)

Are you laughing at me!? Mama this ain't funny!

GAIL. I'm sorry I just feel so serene.

I feel so good right now, honey, and you're just freaking out and it's funny to me and I'm so sorry.

...

...

I should've lived like this.

I'm glad I get to die like this but I should've lived like this, Joy.

Joy, you should live like this.

JOY. Like what?

GAIL. Like *this*.

JOY. I don't know what you mean, Mama.

GAIL. Like if all your worries was ice cream.

How can you eat all that ice cream before it melts?

You can't.

JOY. Just like that, huh?

GAIL. Just like that.

JOY. How?

GAIL. You right there, baby.

You there, you just gotta *know* you there.

Try not to let the responsibility get to you too much, okay?

Easy for me to say now.

But don't let it get to you.

JOY. ...

GAIL. However many eggs you choose to set aside, that's the right choice.

Okay?

JOY. ...

...

...

    (**GAIL** *opens the door.*)

HA-HA. Where you going Grandma?

...

GAIL. ...

For a drive.

...

See y'all tonight.

    (**GAIL** *exits.*)

    (*A silence.*)

    (**JOY** *enters the bedroom.*)

    (*She takes the tobacco pipe out of the dresser drawer. She has some trouble lighting it, but eventually it takes.*)

    (*She smokes for a short moment.*)

JOY. Symphony, may I have a word with you, dear?

SYMPHONY. Of course.

    (**SYMPHONY** *enters the bedroom.*)

JOY. Please have a seat, I'll just be a minute.

    (**JOY** *smokes.*)

    (*In the main room,* **EARLY** *motions* **HA-HA** *to sit next to her.*)

EARLY. Are you doin' the thing yet?

HA-HA. We just met, Great Grandma.

EARLY. So you not? You not doin' the thing?

HA-HA. We just met *today*, Great Grandma.

EARLY. You'll figure it out. I'm confident you will.

HA-HA. ...

Maybe I'll wait.

EARLY. Wait?

HA-HA. Ain't it like...fornication?

EARLY. Well, yes. It is.

HA-HA. I thought I wasn't supposed to do that?

EARLY. You ain't. You ain't supposed to do that.

HA-HA. So if I ain't supposed to do that...

EARLY. Well, you also ain't expected to not do all the things you ain't supposed to do.

HA-HA. Why?

EARLY. Don't be asking me *why*. I didn't make the world.

HA-HA. ...

Well, I'm gonna do the right thing.

EARLY. Don't be talkin' to me about right things.

You know what the matter with you is, Ha-Ha?

You read too much.

You read everything and don't understand none of it.

HA-HA. ...

I understand a lot.

EARLY. ...

Bring me that cup of tea, would you?

(**HA-HA** *brings* **EARLY** *a cup of tea.*)

You're the only one who can make tea like this. Did you know that Ha-Ha? You're the only one who makes it just like this. Have you had any?

HA-HA. No.

EARLY. Pour yourself a cup and sit with me. And we gonna sip it together. And we ain't gonna say nothin'.

(**HA-HA** *pours himself a cup of tea...*)

(*In the bedroom,* **JOY** *continues to smoke.*)

JOY. How did you and Ha-Ha meet?

SYMPHONY. If I did something wrong I really apologize.

JOY. How'd you meet?

SYMPHONY. In Carbondale.

I was buying coffee and he was right behind me and he bought a hot chocolate. And I smiled at him, I guess. I didn't mean anything by it, he just looked so sweet.

And then he asked me if I would be his friend. And, knee-jerk reaction, I just said, "Of course, friends for life!" And then, like, someone stole my car –

JOY. What?

SYMPHONY. Yeah, I get out to the parking lot and my car is gone.

Which, actually, wasn't a total surprise because, um, there's just,

Some stuff that has been going wrong in terms of

My life

It's complicated, I'm working it out, just...

JOY. So Ha-Ha offered you a ride.

SYMPHONY. Yeah! So he's driving me over to a friend's place. And I'm like, Where are you from, what do you do? And he starts talking about his house with no address in the middle of the woods that his great grandparents built, and I said, No you've got to be kidding me, and he said, No, like I'm not kidding, and I said, Well, I have to *see* it. I don't believe you I need to see it.

And he said, Okay.

JOY. ...

...

I can't stand the taste of tobacco

SYMPHONY. Yeah, it's acquired.

>   *(The pipe goes out.)*

JOY. Can't seem to keep this thing lit, either.

SYMPHONY. Sometimes if you stuff it too full, like if it's too dense in there / it won't –

JOY. I'm a terrible mother!

SYMPHONY. What? No you're not.

JOY. Yes, I am. Yes I am yes I am yes I am.

>   *(**SYMPHONY** reaches into her handbag and pulls out a small bag of potato chips. She offers it to **JOY**.)*

...

SYMPHONY. Sorry.

I always carry around a bag of chips for, like, emotional emergencies.

I'm weird. Never mind.

>   *(**JOY** takes the chips, opens them, and eats half the bag.)*

JOY. I'm supposed to be able to run this house. And now you're here and you're gonna... oh God.

SYMPHONY. What am I gonna do?

JOY. Okay, so the thing you need to know about Ha-Ha... well there's a lot of things to know. He's, um, he's very, uh...

SYMPHONY. Ticklish.

JOY. Sorry?

SYMPHONY. He's very ticklish.

JOY. ...

Yes, / he is –

SYMPHONY. Really, Ha-Ha and I just met. We're not like... we haven't, like / done anything, like –

JOY. Okay, that's fine you don't / need to –

SYMPHONY. I just want you to know that I would never disrespect your home or your family. It feels like, Church or something in here.

...

It's lovely here.

JOY. Does that mean you would you like to stay the night?

SYMPHONY. Oh!

I mean, I have work in the morning.

JOY. Well, the truck is gone. My mother took the truck.

SYMPHONY. She said she'd be back?

JOY. Yes. But I don't think the truck is gonna make it. We'll have to get it towed to the shop most likely.

SYMPHONY. ...

Is this a kidnapping?

JOY. No,

It's...

It's the way things go here.

SYMPHONY. ...Alright.

JOY. Gail was a rock. You know? She may not have been a natural born rock but she damnsure made herself into one. And I don't know how, Symphony. I don't know how she did it. And even if I did know,

...

Well I don't. I don't and maybe that's the whole point.

Are you a rock, Symphony?

Could you be if you had to?

SYMPHONY. ...

I used to have a rock *collection*.

JOY. Okay, that's...okay, good.

SYMPHONY. I ended up giving most of them away, though.

JOY. You lost interest?

SYMPHONY. No, it just,

It didn't make sense anymore. Like that's not where rocks belong. A bunch of glass jars?

So I found special places for them.

JOY. Where?

SYMPHONY. I don't know. Ravines. Creeks. Ponds. Whatever felt right for whatever particular rock.

JOY. ...

I see why you and Ha-Ha get each other so well.

SYMPHONY. ...

JOY. You can sleep on the sofa.

Ha-Ha usually sleeps on the floor out there in his sleeping bag.

And Great Grandma Early, she has to sleep in her chair, because of her back. So she'll be out there next to you. I hope you don't mind.

SYMPHONY. Um...sure.

JOY. And I'll be...

I'll be in here, I guess.

SYMPHONY. ...

JOY. Would you mind helping me change the sheets?

There's some fresh linens in the bottom drawer of that dresser, if you could pull them out.

> (*JOY pulls the sheets off of her mother's bed and places them in a laundry basket.* **SYMPHONY** *stands as if at attention, holding the clean sheets.*)
>
> (**JOY** *and* **SYMPHONY** *make the bed together.*)

Epilogue

(Night. Starlight through the trees.)

*(**SYMPHONY** sleeps on the sofa bed.)*

*(**HA-HA** sleeps on the floor in his sleeping bag.)*

*(**EARLY** sleeps stretched out on her easy chair.)*

*(**JOY** sleeps on the bed in the bedroom.)*

*(Two shadowed figures enter through the front door. These are **GAIL** and **WALKING MAN**.)*

*(**WALKING MAN** tucks in **EARLY** and **HA-HA**. He goes to the sofa and begins to tuck in **SYMPHONY**.)*

GAIL. That ain't your daughter.

WALKING MAN. ...

Whoa! My bad.

*(**WALKING MAN** enters the bedroom. He pulls the tobacco pipe out of the dresser drawer. He fills it with tobacco.)*

(He takes a lighter off of the dresser and lights it.)

(He lights the pipe and smokes.)

*(**GAIL** enters the bedroom and tucks **JOY** in.)*

JOY. ...Mama?

GAIL. Go 'head back to sleep, baby.

JOY. Love you, mama...

> *(**WALKING MAN** and **GAIL** go back into the main room.)*
>
> *(**WALKING MAN** places his lighter and the still smoldering pipe on the table.)*
>
> *(**GAIL** and **WALKING MAN** exit, closing the door behind them.)*
>
> *(**SYMPHONY** sits up.)*
>
> *(She picks up the pipe.)*
>
> *(She smokes.)*

SYMPHONY. For the record:

I actually was surprised that someone stole my car.

It's a sedan with two hundred thousand miles on it and a missing driver's side window.

I acted like I had it coming because

It's just easier to blame things on yourself.

...

But hey.

If I still had my car

Would I ever have made it here?

> *(**SYMPHONY** places the pipe back on the table.)*
>
> *(**SYMPHONY** looks, long, at **EARLY**, who remains asleep in her chair.)*

I have a million questions for you, ma'am.

> *(**SYMPHONY** picks up the lighter.)*

(She opens its lid and, to her surprise, the lighter seems to light itself.)

(The fire burns her hand and she closes it quickly.)

(She opens the lighter again, more carefully this time.)

(Again, the flame sprouts up.)

(It burns high and bright.)

End of Play

Part 2:
Walking Man

PART 2: WALKING MAN was originally produced in New York City by Roundabout Theatre Company in association with New York Theatre Workshop at the Harold and Miriam Steinberg Center for Theatre / Laura Pels Theatre on October 11, 2023. The performance was directed by Patricia McGregor, with set design by Arnulfo Maldonado, lighting design by Stacey Derosier, costume design by Emilio Sosa, and original music and sound design by Marc Anthony Thompson. The production stage manager was Katie Ailinger. The cast was as follows:

WALKING MAN	Jon Michael Hill
EARLY	Nicole Ari Parker
CRAZY EDDIE	Daniel J. Watts
DAX	Lance Coadie Williams
CLYDETTE	Lizan Mitchell
REGINALD	Jerome Preston Bates
GAIL	Jessica Frances Dukes

CHARACTERS

WALKING MAN – (M, 20s) An aimless wanderer, settled once again in his childhood home.

EARLY – (W, 40s) Walking Man's mother.

CRAZY EDDIE – (M, 40s) Early's husband.

DAX – (M, 40s) Crazy Eddie's younger brother.

CLYDETTE – (W, 60s-70s) A ghost. Early's mother.

REGINALD – (M, 60s-70s) A ghost. Early's father.

GAIL – (W, 20s) A young woman from a nearby town.

SETTING

A small clearing in a big forest in southern Illinois,
in which is nestled a makeshift house.

TIME

Summer. The 1970s.

AUTHOR'S NOTE

An ellipsis line in the dialogue [...] represents a pause, a beat or perhaps a physical action.

When a line of dialogue ends in a dash [–] this means the next line comes right on top of it, perhaps with an overlap.

Where an overlap is needed in a specific place, it is marked by a slash [/].

One

(Morning. Summer.)

(A small clearing in a big forest.)

(In the clearing we see the exterior of a small house, made from scrap lumber.)

(A few steps away from the house is a fresh pile of dirt. Someone has been digging a hole.)

(There is one particularly large tree at the edge of the clearing.)

(Also in the clearing is a small, wooden structure with three low walls and no roof. This is a washing station. For people, clothes, dishes, etc.)

*(**WALKING MAN** enters. He is a young man in his early twenties. Lean but sturdy. He pulls a wagon, in which are several buckets of water.)*

(Exhausted from the long haul, he approaches the house and moves to open the door, but before he can reach it, someone swings it open from the inside, hitting him in the face.)

*(The opener of the door is **EARLY**, his mother. She is youthful but weathered.)*

WALKING MAN. Ow!

EARLY. I ain't break your nose, did I?

WALKING MAN. My nose is fine, you got me in my ear.

EARLY. Good.

WALKING MAN. Think you busted my eardrum.

EARLY. What you need an eardrum for? You don't be hearin' me any damn way.

WALKING MAN. ...

I brought water up.

EARLY. Actin' like you been at the river.

WALKING MAN. I *was* at the river.

This here is river water.

EARLY. All night, Walking Man? It took you all night to walk to the river and back?

WALKING MAN. It's nice outside.

It's *space* out here.

EARLY. Who you been talkin' to out there?

WALKING MAN. Nobody.

EARLY. Who been talking to *you*?

WALKING MAN. ...

Ain't nobody said nothin' to me.

EARLY. How many times have I told you to stop roaming around / in the middle of the night –

WALKING MAN. Ma, I wasn't roaming around / I was taking a walk –

EARLY. How many times?

WALKING MAN. I couldn't sleep. What I'm s'posed to do, pace up and down the house waking everybody up?

EARLY. Yes.

WALKING MAN. I was restless, so I stepped outside.

It wasn't no long walk.

I'm already back, see?

I know you don't like me taking those long walks. I'm doing my best do make it easy on you. But, Mama, you know me. You know I got to walk.

> (**WALKING MAN** *picks up the buckets, intending to bring them inside.*)
>
> (**EARLY** *remains where she is, blocking the doorway.*)

EARLY. Where you think you goin' now?

WALKING MAN. Bringing the water inside.

> (**EARLY** *takes the buckets and places them inside the doorway.*)
>
> (*She gives the last bucket to* **WALKING MAN.**)

EARLY. Keep that one. That one's for you.

WALKING MAN. What you want me to do with it?

EARLY. Pour the whole thing over your head, turn around three times clockwise, and with each revolution you better be *prayin'.*

WALKING MAN. What I'm s'pose to pray for?

EARLY. Pray for me to let your night-walking ass back in this house.

Pray I feed you today.

WALKING MAN. I can feed myself.

EARLY. Then son, if you don't need me, leave me.

Leave me.

Go on ahead. Right now.

Go 'head

> (**EARLY** *goes inside and shuts the door.*)
>
> (*A stillness.*)
>
> (**WALKING MAN** *goes to the largest tree in the clearing, sits and leans against it.*)
>
> (*He pulls a tobacco pipe out of his pocket.*)
>
> (*He fills it with tobacco and puts it in his mouth.*)
>
> (*He digs in his pocket for a light.*)
>
> (*He does not have a light.*)
>
> (*The door to the house opens again. Out comes* **CRAZY EDDIE**. *He walks with crutches.*)

CRAZY EDDIE. Where the fuck is my truck?

WALKING MAN. Mornin', pops.

CRAZY EDDIE. Where's my truck?

WALKING MAN. Uncle Dax musta took it.

CRAZY EDDIE. Your uncle is not allowed to drive my truck.

WALKING MAN. He prolly needed to go check on his car. Once his car is fixed up he won't need to borrow the truck no more.

CRAZY EDDIE. How you gonna dig a hole in a man's yard and drive his truck around?

What kind of way is that?

WALKING MAN. Pops, can you toss me a box of matches?

CRAZY EDDIE. No I cannot. 'Cause I don't *keep* no matches.

WALKING MAN. There ain't no matches next to the stove?

CRAZY EDDIE. What you think you know about a stove?

WALKING MAN. I know it don't light itself.

CRAZY EDDIE. Uhuh. That's 'cause you still on that one plus one is two shit.

Sitting there counting on your fingers, while a truck drives away.

WALKING MAN. You never told me don't let nobody drive the truck.

CRAZY EDDIE. Why you got to be told everything? Think for yourself.

WALKING MAN. Think for myself as long as I think like you. That what you mean?

CRAZY EDDIE. Walking Man, let me ask you something:

Do you think you made a point just now?

WALKING MAN. ...

CRAZY EDDIE. 'Cause you said it all loud and you smiled to yourself.

Like you actually thought you said something.

WALKING MAN. Can you please just throw some matches my way?

Mom won't let me in the house.

CRAZY EDDIE. With your stolen pipe. That's my pipe.

WALKING MAN. Pops. I've never once seen you smoke this pipe.

CRAZY EDDIE. Pour that bucket over your head and get to spinnin'!

(**CRAZY EDDIE** *steps back inside the house and closes the door.*)

(**WALKING MAN** *looks at the tree. Its branches sway in the wind.*)

WALKING MAN. How you been?

TREE. ...

WALKING MAN. Sometimes I wish I had roots instead of legs. When you got legs you can't help but feel like you should use 'em. Like you should be on your way somewhere.

If I was like you, I wouldn't have to think about going nowhere.

Wouldn't have to worry about staying nowhere either.

I'd just *be*.

That's all I'm tryna do right now.

For real.

Just let me be.

(**WALKING MAN** *picks up the bucket of water.*)

(*He knocks on the window of the house.*)

(**EARLY**'s *face appears in the window.*)

(**WALKING MAN** *empties the bucket of water onto his head.*)

(*Hands clasped in prayer, he spins himself around, clockwise, three times.*)

(**EARLY** *opens the door.*)

EARLY. Were you really praying?

WALKING MAN. Yes, ma'am.

EARLY. ...

> (**EARLY** *hands* **WALKING MAN** *a folded set of clothes and a towel.*)
>
> (**WALKING MAN** *dries off, changes his shirt and pants.*)
>
> (**EARLY** *goes back inside, briefly, then emerges with a basket full of laundry, which she drops at* **WALKING MAN***'s feet.*)
>
> (*She takes* **WALKING MAN***'s empty water bucket and gives him a full bucket.*)

Do the washing before you come in.

WALKING MAN. Let me come get a match.

EARLY. Why you need to smoke so bad?

WALKING MAN. / Ma –

EARLY. Scrub those night-walking clothes extra hard.

> (**EARLY** *goes back into the house and closes the door.*)
>
> (**WALKING MAN** *brings the laundry and water to the washing station. He pours some of the water in a plastic tub for rinsing. He begins to soap and scrub the laundry from the basket.*)
>
> (*A blue pickup truck enters and parks in the clearing.*)
>
> (*Driving the truck is* **UNCLE DAX**. *He is Crazy Eddie's younger brother, fresh-faced and robust.*)

(He lifts a metal water pump from the truck bed. He places it on the ground next to the pile of dirt.)

(He goes back to the truck and pulls out a bundled-up tent.)

*(He tosses the tent to **WALKING MAN**.)*

DAX. Lay this out for me, nephew-man.

WALKING MAN. What is it?

DAX. It's where I'm sleepin' tonight.

WALKING MAN. Why you sleepin' in a tent, Uncle Dax?

DAX. I like to stretch out.

WALKING MAN. How 'bout I sleep in the tent and you can have the living room to yourself?

*(The door to the house opens and **CRAZY EDDIE** emerges.)*

CRAZY EDDIE. *(Re: the truck.)* You pulled it in too far.

DAX. That's where it was.

CRAZY EDDIE. Gimmie the keys, I need to move it.

DAX. I'll move it.

CRAZY EDDIE. Nah, ah, no. You've already demonstrated that you don't know where it goes.

*(**CRAZY EDDIE** walks to the truck.)*

(He presses his ear to the hood.)

(He listens for a while.)

...

You was drivin' too slow.

DAX. ...

CRAZY EDDIE. *(Listens again.)* ...

You was drivin' all night.

Wasn't you.

Don't lie, now. Don't you try and lie to Crazy Eddie.

DAX. I had to go up to Culver City.

CRAZY EDDIE. What for?

DAX. For that pump.

> (**CRAZY EDDIE** *stares at the water pump.*)

CRAZY EDDIE. We don't have no water line out here.

DAX. I'll find one.

CRAZY EDDIE. You out your damn mind.

DAX. So what if I am?

CRAZY EDDIE. Nastyass Culver City dirt on my grill. Take your own damn car to Culver City.

DAX. My car's still in the shop. They waitin' on bolts. Bolts to replace the wheel.

CRAZY EDDIE. Scrapyard right across the street. And they waitin on *bolts*.

DAX. Scrapyard don't got what they need. It's custom.

CRAZY EDDIE. What they need is a custom foot up they ass. That's what they waitin' on. I should drive up there my *damn*self. You wait for them and they bolts you be waitin' forever.

Toss me the keys.

> (**EARLY** *comes out of the house.*)

...

EARLY. Dax, give the keys to me.

CRAZY EDDIE. Hold on just a minute, now, just a minute,

Just hold on a minute.

Hold on a minute now.

Early.

I'll back the truck into its *spot*,

And I'll give the keys to you.

EARLY. ...

DAX. Ed you know we can't have you driving.

CRAZY EDDIE. Y'all don't know I been practicing. I can get her down to the big road and back without a scratch.

EARLY. We know you can, Edward.

CRAZY EDDIE. Then you should know I can park.

EARLY. ...

DAX. ...

CRAZY EDDIE. Park it right next time. Or I will.

>   (**CRAZY EDDIE** *gets winded and leans on something.*)

WALKING MAN. Pops you alright?

CRAZY EDDIE. *(Registering everyone's concern.)* Back up, give me some air.

Talkin' sense into y'all is a day's work and then some.

>   (**WALKING MAN** *unfolds Dax's tent and lays it out on the grass.*)

EARLY. *(To **WALKING MAN**.)* What's that for?

WALKING MAN. This Uncle Dax's tent.

EARLY. ...

DAX. Want to get as much of this fresh air as I can while I'm here.

EARLY. The sofa's not comfortable enough for you? Let it break in a little.

DAX. All due respect: That thing don't need to break in. That thing *broke*.

CRAZY EDDIE. You know something?

I ain't had a nap since '63.

Was it '63?

DAX. Why not, you ain't got nothin' else to do around here –

CRAZY EDDIE. / I got plenty to do –

DAX. What, you too busy watchin' grass grow to take a nap –

> (**EARLY** *raises her hand and perks her ears. All fall silent and look at her.*)

EARLY. ...

I think I hear a turkey out back.

...

> (*They all listen.*)
>
> (*Nobody hears anything.*)

WALKING MAN. I don't hear nothing –

EARLY. Shhh.

> (**EARLY** *walks around the house and peeks behind it. She snaps her head back. This is a one-woman, barehanded SWAT operation.*)
>
> (*She slowly peeks around the wall again.*)

> *(And she springs into action, disappearing behind the house.)*
>
> *(The sound of a turkey gobbling and flapping its wings.)*
>
> *(Silence.)*
>
> *(...)*
>
> *(...)*
>
> *(**EARLY** returns, holding a wild turkey by its limp neck.)*
>
> *(**EARLY** hands the turkey to **WALKING MAN**.)*

Start getting her ready.

> *(**WALKING MAN** takes the turkey to a post and ties it up by the feet.)*
>
> *(**EARLY** takes a long, deep breath.)*

Thank you Lord for sending this special dinner our way.

We wasn't expecting it. We wasn't even askin' for it. But in your Wisdom, you knew. You knew.

And we thank you, Lord, for the blessing of family. We thank you for keeping Walking Man safe at home where he belongs.

And we thank you for sending our Dax here to see us.

Lord, we are / so grateful –

DAX. Oh, uh...

EARLY. ...

DAX. Sorry.

God ain't send me.

Sorry.

EARLY. God ain't send you.

DAX. ...

EARLY. You *here*.

DAX. Yes I am.

EARLY. ...

Alright.

You just *here*.

DAX. Amen.

EARLY. ...

CRAZY EDDIE. I'ma go inside. Take that nap.

Been waitin since '63.

Can't wait no more.

> (**CRAZY EDDIE** *goes into the house.*)

EARLY. ...

I'll boil you some water for that turkey, Walking Man.

WALKING MAN. Okay, ma.

EARLY. ...

...

> (**EARLY** *goes inside and closes the door.*)
>
> (**WALKING MAN** *returns to washing the clothes.*)
>
> (**DAX** *works on the tent.*)

DAX. *(A declaration.)* Walking Man.

WALKING MAN. (*"That's me."*) Yes sir.

DAX. Your old man say you've been spending a lot of time away from home.

WALKING MAN. Nah, I'm back.

DAX. Back from where?

WALKING MAN. Places.

Nowhere in particular.

DAX. ...

I'm a traveler, too. Your old man tell you that?

WALKING MAN. He said you trying to go to Paris.

DAX. That's the plan.

Thought I'd swing by and see y'all on the way.

WALKING MAN. Which Paris?

DAX. ...

WALKING MAN. It's a lot of Parises in the world.

DAX. No it ain't.

WALKING MAN. I've passed by a lot of Parises. There's a Paris up in Edgar county. / There's a Paris down in Tennessee –

DAX. What I look like going up to Edgar county –

WALKING MAN. You got *New* Paris, over in Ohio. You got Paris, Pennsylvania.

DAX. Don't know nothin' about them Parises. I'm talking about *Paris* Paris.

WALKING MAN. Oh, okay. Paris, France.

DAX. I swear to God you your father's son.

Don't make no kinda sense.

WALKING MAN. What you gonna do over there in France?

DAX. Be.

WALKING MAN. Be what?

DAX. Be in Paris motherfucking France.

WALKING MAN. ...

Cool.

DAX. So these trips you been taking. To Nowhere In Particular.

WALKING MAN. I'm only taking short walks now.

DAX. Alright. So, what made you wanna come back home?

WALKING MAN. ...

Is there ever just one reason for anything?

DAX. Philosophizin'! Okay.

WALKING MAN. *Is* there?

DAX. There's a *principal* reason, yes.

Might be a lot of *factors*. Might be a lot of contributing factors or what have you.

WALKING MAN. ...

You think there's such a thing as destiny, Uncle Dax?

DAX. If there is, that motherfucker's a motherfucker.

WALKING MAN. Heard that.

DAX. What's the furthest place you've been?

WALKING MAN. Alaska, I think.

DAX. Alaska!? What, you drove up to Canada dodgin' the draft and you went too far?

WALKING MAN. No.

DAX. *(He has cracked himself up.)* Ha-Haaaaa!

...

WALKING MAN. That's funny, though.

DAX. ...

But you say you wasn't dodgin' the draft.

So was you *there*?

Was you there in 'Nam? That's a helluva lot farther than Alaska.

WALKING MAN. No, sir.

DAX. Got lucky, huh?

WALKING MAN. I ain't have to get lucky. I don't got no birth certificate. Ain't no address on that house.

DAX. Mississippi Goddamn.

...

So you ain't got no social security number. No driver's license.

What you do when the police pull you over?

WALKING MAN. I don't drive.

DAX. You *walked* all the way up to Alaska?

WALKING MAN. Yeah.

DAX. And ain't nobody never stopped you? Ain't nobody detain you?

WALKING MAN. No.

DAX. Okay.

And then after a while you decided, Enough with these whales, enough with these polar bears, I'm comin' home.

WALKING MAN. It wasn't that easy, though.

I got lost a lot.

I always get lost when I go somewhere.

Even last night: I think I'm just gonna go down for a quick dip in the river and next thing I know I'm walkin' all over the forest. Back and forth and back and forth. Passing places I been a hundred times and not recognizing them.

I just be getting lost in my thoughts and that gets me lost on the road. That gets me off the road altogether sometime. And I be seein' these other lost people. At least I think they're people.

DAX. Like who?

WALKING MAN. This couple.

DAX. ...

Elderly couple?

WALKING MAN. Yeah.

DAX. Arm-in-arm?

WALKING MAN. Yeah.

DAX. Lookin' like they got lost on the way to Church?

WALKING MAN. ...

Where you seen 'em at?

DAX. Saw 'em last night, too. Right where you standing.

WALKING MAN. Right here?

DAX. I was out here,

I couldn't sleep, so I made a fire...

WALKING MAN. Yeah?

DAX. And I think I see somethin' out the corner of my eye and I look up.

And there they be.

WALKING MAN. Did you say anything to 'em?

DAX. Of course. We talked. Talked for a while.

WALKING MAN. Who are they?

DAX. I mean,

They damnsure ain't *alive*.

WALKING MAN. ...

What'd they say to you?

DAX. Well, I told them I was here visiting my brother, on my way to Paris, and I was trying to think of a gift for y'all. You know, once I go across the pond, not sure how many times I'll be back this way. This is a special visit. I want you to have something to remember me by. But I didn't know what y'all would want. Or need.

And so they said to me, *What would you like to give them? If you could give them anything at all, what would it be?* And I said, *water*. I'd put a tap out here so y'all don't have to carry those damn buckets around all the time. So y'all don't have to walk half a mile just to wash yourselves.

And they told me, *Alright*.

Told me I just needed to pick a spot and dig a hole. And they told me where to buy the pump. Even gave me some cash. Ain't that crazy?

Gentleman reached all deep into his pocket, Lady opened up her purse, and they put it right into my hands. Real money.

And then they went ahead and shuffled away. Back to church or wherever.

WALKING MAN. And they never told you who they were?

DAX. ...

They scared of your mama.

WALKING MAN. ...

DAX. They kept askin' me, *Is the Lady of the House awake?* And I said, no she's not. But they kept looking at the door.

WALKING MAN. Why they scared of my mama?

DAX. Thought you might tell me.

WALKING MAN. How would I know?

DAX. How would I know how you would know? Deduce some shit, I don't know.

> (**EARLY** *opens the door and places a large pot on the ground.*)

EARLY. Come get this water while it's still hot enough, Walking Man.

> (**WALKING MAN** *picks up the pot.*)

Y'all love to talk don't you?

WALKING MAN. ...

DAX. ...

EARLY. Out here talkin'.

WALKING MAN. ...

DAX. ...

EARLY. Don't let me stop you.

WALKING MAN. ...

DAX. ...

> (**EARLY** *goes back into the house and shuts the door.*)

Maybe we should bring it back to matters of the living for a while.

WALKING MAN. Fine by me.

(**WALKING MAN** *brings the boiling water to where the turkey is hanging. He swirls the bird in the water, then begins pulling off the feathers...*)

DAX. You say you was in Alaska and you got lost on the way home?

WALKING MAN. Yeah. I went south, right? Due south. Or as due south as I could.

Thought I'd stop in California, right? So I was at the beach and all that. And I'm thinkin' damn, it's kinda quiet at this beach.

And then I looked up and I saw a penguin.

DAX. A penguin?

WALKING MAN. Yeah.

DAX. Come on.

WALKING MAN. And then I saw a whole buncha penguins. Like a herd of penguins.

DAX. A *flock*.

WALKING MAN. Penguins ain't no flock –

DAX. It's either a flock or a school. Ain't no *herd* –

WALKING MAN. It's not a flock 'cause they don't *fly*.

DAX. Alright, then it's a school –

WALKING MAN. But they ain't *fish* –

DAX. You gotta pick an argument and follow it through, neph. If you sayin' can't be a flock 'cause they don't fly, then you gotta call 'em a school, 'cause they *swim* –

WALKING MAN. A lotta things swim. Dogs swim. If a bunch of dogs are swimming you gonna call them a *school* of dogs?

DAX. ...

Yes I will.

WALKING MAN. Come on, unc.

DAX. If the motherfuckers are swimmin', yes I will – what you gonna call 'em, a *herd?*

WALKING MAN. ...

Anyway, I'm at the beach. And there's penguins.

DAX. ...

Were they Humboldt penguins?

...

Small and ugly. Look kinda like a vanilla sundae with a beak?

WALKING MAN. Yeah!

DAX. Brotherman I'll bet my bottom dollar you was in South America.

WALKING MAN. ...

I was going *south*.

Guess I overdid it.

>   (**WALKING MAN** *has finished pulling feathers from the turkey. He slices into it with a knife, rather clumsily.*)
>
>   (**DAX** *pauses his work on the tent, observes* **WALKING MAN** *struggling with his job.*)

DAX. Your mama say you been walking since the womb.

WALKING MAN. Mhmmm.

DAX. And you been back how long now?

WALKING MAN. Almost a year.

DAX. Almost a year. Is that a long time, or a short time?

WALKING MAN. Long.

After a while, I'm still? When I'm not on the road? Days feel long. Hours feel long. Even minutes feel long.

DAX. ...

The war's over, you know. They put an end to that shit. So if you wanna go get a birth certificate you should be safe.

WALKING MAN. What I need to certify my birth for? I know I was born.

DAX. It's nice to have ID. As a traveler, you gonna need one sooner or later. Gives you access.

WALKING MAN. And *is* the war over? Or did they just take it off the radio?

...

I was up in Anchorage.

This woman is talkin' to me, right? Her man is in the Navy.

DAX. Uh-oh.

WALKING MAN. What?

DAX. Where was y'all?

WALKING MAN. I don't know. A bar or a saloon / or somethin'.

DAX. What was it called?

WALKING MAN. I don't remember.

DAX. Uhuh, so what you mean to say is, y'all was in her bed getting funky.

WALKING MAN. ...

DAX. Continue.

WALKING MAN. It wasn't like...I didn't premeditate anything –

DAX. Hope you wasn't jiving with her feelings.

WALKING MAN. Me? Please. No way. If anything she was the one jiving *me*.

DAX. If you say so.

WALKING MAN. Come on unc. You know how women be.

DAX. Mhmm, I know how y'all *men* be too.

WALKING MAN. Oh, okay, how's that?

DAX. One day men will say they ready to move mountains for you, next day they'll leave you stranded in a motel in Grand Forks, North Dakota.

And you sit outside on the curb, waiting for them to come back. And you're passing the time, just you and the prairie dogs. And the time keeps on passin' and passin'.

'Cause when men say they gonna *be right back*? That means whatever they *want it* to mean. Could be five minutes. Could be five years. Could be five forevers. That's how men be.

...

WALKING MAN. Oh.

DAX. But not you, though. I'm sure you'd never do that.

WALKING MAN. 'Course not.

DAX. So you say.

WALKING MAN. When I'm leaving, I tell *everybody*.

DAX. Hm. I know your old man didn't teach you that.

WALKING MAN. ...

DAX. So: Navy wife was crying to you about her husband?

WALKING MAN. She said to me, The war ain't never started. It's been started. And they never gonna stop it. It's been goin' on forever. They just decide when they gonna put it on TV. When they gonna put it on the radio. When they gonna put it in print.

And I asked her, I said, does your husband miss you?

And she said she didn't know.

And I said, – this is a good line I think – I said, Well I know for sure that I wouldn't miss you if I was your man.

And she said, Why not?

And I said, I wouldn't ever miss you, 'cause I'd always be with you.

DAX. Okay, that's not bad. She like it?

WALKING MAN. She did like it, but then I think I went a little too –

DAX. Oh no what'd you say –

WALKING MAN. I said, I got a house in the woods where I live with my folks, do you wanna come back there with me and start a family.

She said, No.

I said, Why not?

She said, This place sounds like it's far away.

I said, Yeah it is far away. I thought you might dig that. Thought you might wanna escape from here.

And she got real quiet.

And I could see tears in her eyes.

And I said, Why are you crying.

And she said, I'm not crying.

And I said, Oh. Okay.

And she said, I'm trying not to laugh.

And I said, What's funny?

And she said, Do you even have a car? How'd you get here?

I said, With my feet.

And by now, she's cracking up. I'm saying she can't even talk she laughing so hard.

So I said, Alright. I guess that's that. And I left up out of there.

DAX. ...

WALKING MAN. Don't know what I thought I was looking for in Alaska anyway.

DAX. Sounds to me like you've been a few places,

But you got to learn to pay attention to what you see.

WALKING MAN. What does that mean?

DAX. It means you've walked, but you ain't *travelled* yet.

You done with that turkey?

WALKING MAN. Yeah.

DAX. Come finish putting this tent up. You know how to do this?

WALKING MAN. I gotta finish up the laundry.

DAX. That can wait, this is important.

WALKING MAN. You don't know how to do it?

DAX. 'Course I know how to do it. I wanna see if *you* can do it.

WALKING MAN. ...

DAX. Go ahead, tie it down. Put the stakes in.

I'll do the washing for you.

(**WALKING MAN** *begins working on the tent.*)

(**DAX** *starts washing the clothes.*)

DAX. These your shirts?

(**DAX** *holds up two identical, plain T-shirts.*)

WALKING MAN. Uhuh.

DAX. ...

First thing you need to do when you hit the road again is buy some new shirts.

WALKING MAN. I don't care much how I look. If the shirt is clean and it fits, I'm good.

DAX. Pshhh, how it *looks* is just the beginning, nephew-man. It's about what you feel like. *Who* you feel like. In that shirt. You catch my drift? And you can't know until you've tried on a few.

Now *me?* I like a shirt that makes me feel like I'm James Baldwin.

Jimmy Baldwin knows how to go to Paris.

Jimmy goes across the pond with a pen in one hand, and a cigarette in the other. Talking shit to *everybody*.

WALKING MAN. ...

Uncle Dax.

What if I went with you?

DAX. ...

...

WALKING MAN. I'll get a birth certificate if I have to.

DAX. ...

WALKING MAN. I been alone on all my walks. Crossing paths with people on the road, that ain't the same as setting out with someone by your side. Maybe if I'm with a real traveler, I'll finally figure out what it is I been searching for.

(**EARLY** *opens the door and leans out.*)

EARLY. Breakfast.

(*She goes back into the house.*)

DAX. A traveler needs a destination, Walking Man. You sure you want to borrow mine?

WALKING MAN. ...

You got some matches?

DAX. What for?

(**WALKING MAN** *pulls out his pipe and begins filling it with tobacco.*)

WALKING MAN. Been tryin' to light this pipe all morning.

I'll be in in a minute.

(**DAX** *gives* **WALKING MAN** *a book of matches.*)

(**DAX** *goes into the house.*)

DAX. (*As he shuts the door.*) Walking Man say he need a minute.

(**WALKING MAN** *lights a match.*)

(*A big gust of wind. So big that it bends the limbs of the surrounding trees. The match goes out.*)

(*The wind keeps gusting. He lights another match but it goes out immediately.*)

(**WALKING MAN** *waits a few moments.*)

(No wind.)

(He strikes another match. It doesn't take.)

(He tries another.)

(No fire.)

*(**EARLY** opens the door to the house.)*

EARLY. It's been a minute.

*(**WALKING MAN** walks toward the house.)*

Gonna leave that bird sittin' out here?

*(**WALKING MAN** goes to the washing station and grabs the turkey.)*

(He goes into the house.)

*(**EARLY** looks at the tent.)*

(She looks at the water pump and the hole.)

(She goes back inside and shuts the door.)

Two

(Night.)

*(**DAX** holds an electric lantern.)*

*(Two shadowed figures enter: **REGINALD** and **CLYDETTE**.)*

(They are a distinguished, elderly couple.)

(They are dressed well, as if going to church.)

(They walk arm-in-arm.)

DAX. Hey there.

REGINALD. Mr. Dax?

DAX. Yes, sir.

REGINALD. It's us. Reggie and Clydette.

CLYDETTE. Is the lady of the house awake?

DAX. No, ma'am.

REGINALD. Are you sure?

DAX. I'm sure.

REGINALD. ...

CLYDETTE. ...

DAX. I got the pump.

CLYDETTE. Oh! Well look at that!

DAX. I dug the hole.

REGINALD. Yes, you sure did. It's a good hole, too. Come have a look, Clydette.

CLYDETTE. Yes, a very nice hole.

DAX. Thank you.

So. I'm not sure, uh, you know, I'm not sure what to do now.

REGINALD. ...

CLYDETTE. Well, you have the pump.

DAX. Yes, ma'am.

CLYDETTE. And you have the hole.

DAX. Yes, ma'am.

REGINALD. ...

What's the problem?

DAX. I was looking for a water line.

I mean, Mr. Reggie, you said dig a hole five and a half feet deep, so I did that.

And I thought maybe there was gonna be a hidden pipe or something.

I guess I chose the wrong place.

CLYDETTE. Well, it's right by the house. That's a good spot.

REGINALD. Where else would you put it?

DAX. ...

Where's the water gonna come from?

REGINALD. It's a pump.

CLYDETTE. You pump it. And water comes out. It comes out right here.

DAX. Yes, but there's no water line.

What am I s'pose to connect the pump to?

CLYDETTE. You're not supposed to connect it. You're supposed to plant it.

DAX. How?

REGINALD. You don't know how to plant?

CLYDETTE. Honey, you put it in the hole and you cover it.

DAX. And then what happens?

CLYDETTE. It grows.

DAX. Does it grow a water line?

REGINALD. What's the deal with you and water lines?

CLYDETTE. Reginald, don't be unkind, now.

REGINALD. I'm not being unkind.

DAX. I don't mind I'm just tryna understand –

CLYDETTE. Well, you should mind –

REGINALD. See, Dax don't mind me askin' some questions –

CLYDETTE. Dax, don't be takin' this man's questions.

REGINALD. Dax can take what he wanna take and he can leave what he wanna leave –

CLYDETTE. Take his questions and they'll just keep on comin' 'til you can't take 'em no more –

REGINALD. Alright, Clydette, I won't *ask* no questions.

I'll just talk to you, Dax. And the questions will ask themselves, how's that?

    (**CLYDETTE** *sighs.*)

Dax,

You seem to really love water lines.

They seem important to you.

DAX. Yes, they are.

REGINALD. Talk to me about that.

DAX. There has to be a *source*. A water source. To draw from. That's all.

REGINALD. Well there's trees out here.

DAX. Yes, sir.

REGINALD. Trees need water.

DAX. Yes, sir.

REGINALD. The trees, they've made their own "water lines," if that's what you wanna call them. There are whole cities under this soil. Old cities.

And all cities need water. So you know it's down there.

You go on ahead and give that pump to the old city. And watch what'll happen.

DAX. Okay.

> (**DAX** *places the pump in the hole.*)
>
> (*He gets a shovel and begins shoveling dirt into the hole.*)

CLYDETTE. We'll help.

DAX. You don't have to do that, Miss Clydette.

CLYDETTE. We don't mind.

> (**REGINALD** *and* **CLYDETTE** *help by pushing and kicking dirt into the hole as* **DAX** *uses the shovel.*)
>
> (*They all pat down the earth with their hands.*)
>
> (*They pat.*)
>
> (*They pat.*)
>
> (*They pat.*)

DAX. That's that, huh?

CLYDETTE. Should come up nice.

DAX. How long will it take to grow?

CLYDETTE. Not long at all.

DAX. A few months?

REGINALD. Oh, Lord have mercy, no. No.

DAX. Oh.

REGINALD. Six, seven hours.

CLYDETTE. At the most.

REGINALD. Seven hours at the absolute most.

DAX. Well, alright.

...

Wonderful.

...

I wish there was some way I could repay you.

REGINALD. Oh?

>   (**CLYDETTE** *and* **REGINALD** *stand very still.*)

DAX. ...

Is there something?

REGINALD. Well.

If you're sure you want to offer...

CLYDETTE. Walking Man.

We'd love to talk to Walking Man.

REGINALD. We've been trying to catch his attention but he doesn't want to speak.

Perhaps you could put in a word?

DAX. ...

He's in the front room there.

CLYDETTE. He is?!

DAX. Yes.

I'll send him out.

REGINALD. Thank you, Mr. Dax.

>(**DAX** *enters the house.*)

>(**REGINALD** *and* **CLYDETTE** *hold hands.*)

>(*They stand in great anticipation.*)

>(**WALKING MAN** *comes out.*)

>(*During the following,* **REGINALD** *and* **CLYDETTE** *stand at a distance from* **WALKING MAN.** *They are extremely cautious not to get too close.*)

WALKING MAN. ...

REGINALD. ...

CLYDETTE. ...

WALKING MAN. Y'all okay?

>(*A weight lifted,* **REGINALD** *and* **CLYDETTE** *exhale.*)

CLYDETTE. We're very happy you came out to see us.

WALKING MAN. I been seeing you around.

REGINALD. Yes.

WALKING MAN. Y'all were across the river last night.

CLYDETTE. Yes.

WALKING MAN. Are you going to a funeral or something?

(**REGINALD** *and* **CLYDETTE** *laugh...*)

(And laugh.)

REGINALD. No, no, we don't do that no more.

WALKING MAN. ...

Y'all are spirits.

CLYDETTE. We'd love for you to call us Grandma and Grandpa.

WALKING MAN. Why?

REGINALD. Because that's who we are.

I'm your grandfather. Reginald.

And this is your grandmother, Clydette.

WALKING MAN. ...

...

Y'all must be lost.

REGINALD. Look who's talking! Lost!

As if you're not the lostest boy in the whole wide world!

CLYDETTE. You're almost as lost as we were. Before we passed away.

REGINALD. Oh, and we really did pass away didn't we.

CLYDETTE. It was just like that.

Grief and shame, they can make shadows of you before your time.

REGINALD. Yes they can. And it's very very hard. It's torture. Especially when your wife goes on without you.

CLYDETTE. We're together now, dear, and that's what matters.

REGINALD. And you wake up and she's gone and you're alone with her dead body.

REGINALD. And she just sits there with a little, peaceful grin on her face.

And then when *you* finally die she ain't there to hold your hand –

CLYDETTE. You ain't hold my hand when *I* died –

REGINALD. I was *asleep*!

CLYDETTE. I tried to wake you up you just rolled over and snored –

REGINALD. You shoulda tried harder –

CLYDETTE. I was *having a heart attack, Reginald.*

REGINALD. You hearin' this, Walking Man?

She can't wake me up, but she gonna get outa bed, go to the dresser, change her clothes –

CLYDETTE. Yes I did change my clothes, thank you very much what I look like dyin' in my pajamas?

REGINALD. And die in *my chair*. She got a perfectly good chair, but she gotta die in *my* chair.

CLYDETTE. Ha-haaaaaa yeah, that was wrong of me wasn't it!

REGINALD. That's alright, I forgive you, honey.

CLYDETTE. Thank you, sugar.

...

We're sorry to lay all our stuff out in front of you like this, Walking Man.

But we're family. Sometimes it can't be helped.

You don't get to choose your blood.

Nobody does.

REGINALD. Nobody. Not a single soul. That's the truth.

CLYDETTE. God's honest truth.

WALKING MAN. …

CLYDETTE. You must not blame your mother. That might be too much for her.

WALKING MAN. Blame my mother for what?

REGINALD. …

CLYDETTE. …

REGINALD. For your blood.

CLYDETTE. For the man you've been walking the earth in search of.

REGINALD. For the missing piece of yourself that you will never find.

WALKING MAN. …

> …
>
> Y'all need to go.

> (**CLYDETTE** and **REGINALD** stay where they are.)

CLYDETTE. We're sorry to have to tell you, grandson.

> There's no easy way to learn such a thing.

REGINALD. The man who is your blood…his name is

> Well. Must we speak his name?

CLYDETTE. Von. Von is his name.

REGINALD. Von is what everybody called him, that much we know. And that's as much as we care to know. To be sure, he was the worst of his name.

CLYDETTE. Von, your blood father, he lay with Early

> He lay with Early, our daughter.
>
> …

REGINALD. It was against her will.

WALKING MAN. …

CLYDETTE. That's right.

WALKING MAN. …

…

Y'all don't know what you're talking about. Y'all don't know my mother. Y'all don't know my father. My father is Edward. He's inside right now.

REGINALD. We warned Early about Von. Your blood father.

Warned her not to befriend him.

CLYDETTE. Not only warned. Forbade.

REGINALD. We knew what kind of boy he was. We knew what might happen.

CLYDETTE. …

REGINALD. We were furious with Early. We were beside ourselves.

CLYDETTE. We forgot ourselves.

REGINALD. Yes. Indeed, we did. We forgot ourselves entirely.

CLYDETTE. …

We told Early

…

that her child.

Would never be welcome under our roof.

REGINALD. …

WALKING MAN. …

CLYDETTE. Your mother knows we're near.

REGINALD. She doesn't wish to see our faces.

CLYDETTE. We've learned to pitch our voices on the wind

REGINALD. Yes, we sing to her. We can't stay away.

CLYDETTE. No, we can't. Not from her. And certainly not from you.

REGINALD. We've seen you grow up, Walking Man.

Being your grandparents is,

Well,

It's our favorite thing to be.

CLYDETTE. Oh, by far. You are beyond wonderful.

REGINALD. We've always tried our best to guide you home

When you get lost like you do.

CLYDETTE. Yes.

REGINALD. Yes.

But now we need to ask you to wander no more.

CLYDETTE. Stay with Early. Hold her up. Keep her safe.

REGINALD. Be our arms' embrace

CLYDETTE. And our broken hearts' encompassment.

WALKING MAN. …

My mother said she didn't know her parents.

My mother said she was an orphan.

CLYDETTE. …

REGINALD. …

CLYDETTE. Reginald, do you have that light?

*(**REGINALD** pulls a lighter from his pocket.)*

*(He lights it and holds the lit flame out to **WALKING MAN**.)*

REGINALD. May we light your pipe, Walking Man?

WALKING MAN. ...

REGINALD. We've seen you trying to smoke the last few days.

Seems like every time you have a minute to sit down, you don't have any fire.

WALKING MAN. ...

No, thank you.

REGINALD. Well, here. Take the lighter for later.

It's a special one. Never runs out of fuel.

Works every time. Nice high flame.

Makes your life just a little easier.

Lightens your load a little bit.

...

Would you like it?

> (**REGINALD** *begins to approach.*)

> (**WALKING MAN** *steps back.*)

CLYDETTE. You don't have to take it.

It's alright.

WALKING MAN. ...

CLYDETTE. Reginald. He doesn't have to take it.

> (**REGINALD** *puts the lighter back in his pocket.*)

REGINALD. We sure are proud of you, Walking Man.

CLYDETTE. We love you very much.

Very, very much.

> (**WALKING MAN** *does not respond.*)

(**CLYDETTE** *and* **REGINALD** *exit together.*)

WALKING MAN. ...

...

...

(**DAX** *and* **CRAZY EDDIE** *come out of the house.*)

CRAZY EDDIE. You alright, Walking Man. You alright.

WALKING MAN. Y'all hear that?

DAX. Walking Man, come on inside.

WALKING MAN. ...

CRAZY EDDIE. Listen to your uncle.

Come in the house, now. It's late.

...

WALKING MAN. Is Mama awake?

CRAZY EDDIE. She in bed.

WALKING MAN. ...

Did she hear that?

CRAZY EDDIE. ...

DAX. Sorry I had to wake you up, Walking Man.

...

They asked for you.

...

They ain't mean no harm.

WALKING MAN. Y'all should go inside. Pops, you got to rest.

Uncle Dax, make sure Pops gets his rest.

CRAZY EDDIE. I'll rest if you rest, how about that?

WALKING MAN. ...

CRAZY EDDIE. Don't be pacing up and down like that.

DAX. Like you about to fight somebody.

CRAZY EDDIE. Who you trying to fight, Walking Man?

DAX. For real. Ain't nobody in these woods tryna fight you.

CRAZY EDDIE. You alright.

You alright, come on inside.

WALKING MAN. Y'all see me laughing?

DAX. Walking Man, be cool.

WALKING MAN. Where is he?

CRAZY EDDIE. ...

DAX. ...

WALKING MAN. Let me find my blood father tonight.

And tonight he gonna die.

CRAZY EDDIE. You can't do that, Walking Man.

WALKING MAN. All y'all got to do is point. Point to where he stay, and I'll go. I'll find him.

DAX. No, Walking Man, you won't.

WALKING MAN. ...

CRAZY EDDIE. Your mother is not the only person that man hurt.

WALKING MAN. ...

CRAZY EDDIE. People talk.

And when they talk enough. At some point. Somebody takes care of it.

WALKING MAN. He's already dead?

My blood father's already dead?

CRAZY EDDIE. …

That's right.

WALKING MAN. How you know?

How you know for sure?

CRAZY EDDIE. …

WALKING MAN. Did you kill him?

CRAZY EDDIE. No, I did not.

WALKING MAN. Then you don't know.

DAX. Yes we do.

WALKING MAN. Did you kill him, Uncle Dax?

DAX. No, I did not.

WALKING MAN. Then point me where to go. Point me where to go and I'll make sure.

DAX. Come on inside the house.

WALKING MAN. Point.

Point me where to go.

CRAZY EDDIE. …

No I will not.

If you need to go, then that's what you gonna do. But I ain't pointing you no way.

I ain't no passerby on your road to be pointing you toward whatever you say.

…

You don't want to go to war, Walking Man.

You go to war, and the war gonna come home with you.

I came home and the war was right by my side.

CRAZY EDDIE. I tried to walk away from it.

Tried to shrug it off.

Tried to laugh it away.

Finally I had to say, alright. Okay.

You here to stay. But I'm gonna find my peace any damn way. I'm gonna have so much motherfucking peace, war ain't gonna know no breathing room.

I didn't raise you to be the son of my war.

I raised you to be the son of my peace.

You my peace.

...

(**CRAZY EDDIE** *gets lightheaded and nearly falls.* **DAX** *holds him up.*)

DAX. Easy, Ed, easy.

(**CRAZY EDDIE** *shrugs* **DAX** *off.*)

CRAZY EDDIE. Dax, why don't you come sleep inside.

Let's leave the tent for Walking Man so he can get some air.

WALKING MAN. I don't need no air.

I need to make sure that man is in his grave.

CRAZY EDDIE. We'll talk about it in the morning. We'll talk in the light of day. When we've all had some sleep.

(**CRAZY EDDIE** *goes into the house.*)

WALKING MAN. ...

DAX. It feels like you only got but two choices, sometime.

Stop or go. Stay or leave. Live or die.

But there's always something else.

There's always something in the middle.

...

You and I both know you ain't getting no sleep tonight. Alright.

My old man used to tell me, If you can't get your thoughts together, go think by the water.

...

Go to the river, Walking Man.

Don't go nowhere else 'til you've heard what the river has to say.

And from there, go your way.

>   (**DAX** *goes into the house.*)

WALKING MAN. ...

...

...

>   (**WALKING MAN** *exits.*)

Three

(Morning.)

(The water pump is now fully grown.)

*(**EARLY** comes out of the house.)*

(She goes to the tent.)

EARLY. Walking Man?

Walking Man you in there?

*(**EARLY** opens the tent. No one is there.)*

*(**EARLY** sees the water pump.)*

(She walks to it, and stands looking at it from a safe distance.)

…

…

…

*(**EARLY** approaches the pump.)*

(She reaches out and touches it.)

(She raises and lowers the handle.)

(Water comes out of the spout.)

…

…

…

*(**DAX** comes out of the house.)*

DAX. ...

Morning.

EARLY. ...

> *(DAX sees the pump.)*

DAX. Do it work?

EARLY. You know where Walking Man got off to?

DAX. If he's not in the tent, he must be down by the river.

He had a hard time sleeping last night.

I told him don't do nothing out of hand – just go down by the river.

Walking Man listens.

He got to do things his own way, but he knows how to listen.

He's not far.

He's by the river.

EARLY. ...

I'll go down there and make sure.

> *(EARLY exits.)*
>
> *(DAX lights a cigarette.)*
>
> *(CRAZY EDDIE ambles out of the house.)*
>
> *(He stares at DAX and the pump.)*

DAX. Look who's up and breathing.

> *(DAX pumps the handle of the water pump.)*
>
> *(Water flows out.)*
>
> *(DAX fills a cup and offers it to CRAZY EDDIE.)*

CRAZY EDDIE. ...

What the hell you go and do?!

DAX. Told you I'd figure it out.

>   (**CRAZY EDDIE** *drinks the water.*)

CRAZY EDDIE. I can't be takin' naps no more.

DAX. You still dizzy? You could barely stand last night.

CRAZY EDDIE. I stand when I stand and I fall when I fall. That's how it is with me now.

DAX. ...

CRAZY EDDIE. Water line was right beneath our feet all these years. And you come in and you find it right away.

DAX. ...

CRAZY EDDIE. Where Early at?

DAX. She went out looking for Walking Man.

CRAZY EDDIE. *(Re: the pump.)* She seen this?

DAX. She seen it.

>   (**DAX** *begins taking down his tent and folding it up.*)

I'm gonna walk on up to the mechanic. If they ain't done yet, like you said, they need a swift kick in the ass.

CRAZY EDDIE. You can't wait to get outa here, huh?

DAX. Don't go there, Ed.

CRAZY EDDIE. Why don't you stay a while? France ain't going nowhere.

DAX. Stay for what?

I know you don't appreciate me digging up your yard.

CRAZY EDDIE. You don't like it when Early be praying over you, huh?

Talking about *God ain't send me.*

DAX. I said God ain't send me because I sent me. What I look like asking God to make my travel arrangements?

CRAZY EDDIE. Heard that.

DAX. I don't mind if folks want to pray. But I'll be damned if you speak to God for me. I got my own tongue. My own mind. And my own heart. And I be praying all the time. I pray a lot of ways. I prefer to pray without speaking, when I can. When I open up my mouth to speak to God, first thing I think is, Damn. Where do I even begin? Where, God, do I even begin?

CRAZY EDDIE. So you off to Paris. Sounds like that's your next beginning.

Paris, France.

DAX. That's where I'm headed.

CRAZY EDDIE. City of love.

DAX. That's what some folks call it.

CRAZY EDDIE. That what you call it?

Is love the new beginning you're after?

You going to Paris for love?

DAX. When I'm in love's own city, I won't have to look for love. In love's city, love finds *you.*

I might even mess around and find me, too.

CRAZY EDDIE. …

Oh. Alright.

You gonna find yourself over there in France. Over there in Paris France you gonna find *you.*

DAX. Why you want me to stay? Thought you couldn't stand me driving your truck, parking in the wrong place. Thought you couldn't wait for me to be up out of here.

CRAZY EDDIE. That was yesterday. This is today. And you leaving. Guess I see things in another light now.

DAX. Well, hey. At least I'm saying goodbye.

CRAZY EDDIE. ...

Okay. Alright,

Okay, I alright, I see.

You still mad at me for coming out here? For staying out here?

DAX. No.

CRAZY EDDIE. What then? 'Cause you sure as shit mad at something.

DAX. Be who you be.

Do what you do.

But damn. Tell somebody. The people you claim to love: tell them what's going on. Don't send a postcard three years later and act like everything's cool. Like I'm supposed to pretend you didn't up and disappear on everyone.

CRAZY EDDIE. You right.

I went my way way back when. And we never talk about it.

DAX. ...

I don't suppose there's a whole lot to talk about.

You go down a path, the path do the talking for you.

CRAZY EDDIE. ...

Let's go into town, you and me.

You can drive.

Maybe if we on the way somewhere, we'll hear each other better.

DAX. If you say so.

CRAZY EDDIE. ...

Early got water now. Thanks to you.

That's ten extra years on her life.

DAX. Her life, but not yours?

CRAZY EDDIE. I ain't tryna think about that. All this sleeping and falling. You know this ain't me. Let's not talk about my life.

DAX. ...

CRAZY EDDIE. Hold on, I need to get something.

DAX. Tell me where it is I'll get it.

CRAZY EDDIE. I'ma get it wait right there.

> (**CRAZY EDDIE** *goes to the house.*)

> (**CRAZY EDDIE** *comes back out. He holds a coin.*)

I been saving this. From the war. Didn't know quite what I was saving it for. But now I do.

> (**CRAZY EDDIE** *gives the coin to* **DAX**.)

DAX. ...

CRAZY EDDIE. That's a franc, right there. We ain't gonna spend it tonight. That's yours for when you get to France.

DAX. That's what I figured.

CRAZY EDDIE. It ain't worth a whole lot. But at least you'll have something to start with. That franc been out here as long as I have. That coin is from two worlds now. Maybe that'll double your luck when you get to Paris. Get your new beginning off on the right track.

DAX. ...

CRAZY EDDIE. ...

DAX. What you want to do in town?

(**CRAZY EDDIE** *scribbles out a note for* **EARLY**, *and leaves it on the door.*)

CRAZY EDDIE. Don't know. Don't really matter. Somewhere where we can talk shit 'til the sun come up. Let's make it a long goodbye, this time, since I skipped the last one.

DAX. What's Early gonna say when she come back and we ain't here?

CRAZY EDDIE. Early and Walking Man got some things they need to talk about. Let's leave them to it.

DAX. If you say so –

CRAZY EDDIE. I done said so get your slow ass in this truck –

DAX. I still got your keys I'll go as slow as I damnwell please –

CRAZY EDDIE. I could hotwire this thing in three seconds –

DAX. Like hell you could –

CRAZY EDDIE. Five seconds tops –

DAX. That oldass truck / you lucky it starts at all –

CRAZY EDDIE. This truck ain't old,

DAX. That truck was old as the hills when you got it, and it's even older now. You drive that truck over a hill and it's gonna say, Damn! This motherfucker older than me!

CRAZY EDDIE. I just put a new engine in –

DAX. That's the same shit you said when you first bought it how many engines / you put in this thing –

CRAZY EDDIE. Don't be counting my engines, motherfucker, get in and drive!

> (**CRAZY EDDIE** and **DAX** get into the truck. **DAX** behind the wheel. **CRAZY EDDIE** and **DAX** drive off)
>
> (**WALKING MAN** enters, followed by **EARLY**.)
>
> (**WALKING MAN** carries a long stick.)

EARLY. Walking Man, say something to me.

WALKING MAN. ...

EARLY. Walking Man you forgot how to speak?

WALKING MAN. Got somebody I need to hunt.

EARLY. Who do you think you're going to hunt?

WALKING MAN. My blood.

EARLY. ...

WALKING MAN. The man I been looking for without knowing it.

Pops and Uncle Dax tell me he already dead.

EARLY. ...

WALKING MAN. I didn't know what to do. So I went to the river.

And I found my answer.

>(**WALKING MAN** *begins sharpening the point of his stick with a knife.*)

EARLY. I cried that river myself, Walking Man.

Don't forget that.

Wasn't no water in that riverbed when I got here. And I cried into it, and it ain't stopped flowing since.

And that river gave me you.

That river kept me alive. And it kept you alive, too.

You: my comfort and my miracle.

WALKING MAN. *(Holding up his stick.)* I found this by the river, too.

EARLY. ...

WALKING MAN. If I can't kill him, I know can find someone like him.

I can find someone for my spear.

EARLY. ...

WALKING MAN. How many men like my blood father are there in the world?

Every town must have them. Every city must have them.

And there's no city on the earth I can't reach.

EARLY. Walking Man this ain't you talkin'. Stop.

WALKING MAN. How many men you think I can collect on my spear at once?

How many spears you think I'm gonna need?

...

>(**EARLY** *grabs* **WALKING MAN**'s *spear.* **WALKING MAN** *pulls it away.*)

>   *(She grabs at it again, claws at **WALKING MAN**'s hands and arms. He pushes her off.)*
>
>   *(**WALKING MAN** resumes sharpening his spear.)*

EARLY. ...

I don't like how you look.

Sharpening that thing.

WALKING MAN. ...

EARLY. You ain't never looked like that before.

WALKING MAN. I don't care what I look like.

>   *(**EARLY**, shocked, looks around to regain her bearings.)*
>
>   *(She notices that the truck is gone.)*

EARLY. ...

...

EDWARD!?

...

Where did they go?

Where did they go where did they go where did they go?

EDWARD!?

DAX!?

EDWARD!?

...

I'm going to look for your father.

Your living father, Walking Man.

WALKING MAN. ...

EARLY. ...

These trees have been good to us.

You gonna make spears out of all of them?

You want a spear for every wrong that's been done?

...

This place will be a desert.

...

WALKING MAN. One way or another, mMma. I will have my blood.

EARLY. Then I will be alone.

(**EARLY** *exits.*)

WALKING MAN. ...

...

...

(**WALKING MAN** *continues carving his spear.*)

(*Hours pass. From day to night.* **WALKING MAN** *readies himself to leave.*)

Four

(Night.)

(**WALKING MAN**, *holding his spear and a backpack, stands outside the house. He's preparing to set out.*)

(A single shadowed figure enters the clearing.)

(This is **GAIL**, *a young woman. She holds an ignited lighter in her hand.)*

(She stands at a distance from the house and watches it.)

(**WALKING MAN** *sees* **GAIL**, *but does not approach her.*)

WALKING MAN. Are you alive or dead?

GAIL. Who, me?

WALKING MAN. Yes.

GAIL. Alive.

WALKING MAN. You sure?

GAIL. Far as I know.

WALKING MAN. You lost?

GAIL. Don't think so.

Do you have something for me to light?

WALKING MAN. Say what?

GAIL. I have a lighter. Do you have something for me to light? Maybe that sharp stick you got? The flame is starting to burn my hand.

(**WALKING MAN** *digs in his pockets for his pipe.*)

GAIL. It really hurts.

(**WALKING MAN** *begins stuffing his pipe with tobacco.*)

Ow.

Ouch!

WALKING MAN. Let it go and start it up again.

GAIL. I don't want the fire to be sad.

(**GAIL** *holds the flame to the pipe.* **WALKING MAN** *inhales.*)

WALKING MAN. You don't want the fire to be sad?

Are you forreal?

GAIL. How would you feel? If you were a fire. And you were burning yourself out. And nobody used you for anything?

WALKING MAN. Where you from, Fire Lady?

GAIL. My name ain't Fire Lady.

WALKING MAN. What I'm s'pose to call you?

GAIL. Gail.

WALKING MAN. Gale like the wind?

GAIL. Gail like Abigail. Short for Abigail.

WALKING MAN. It's okay if I call you Gale like the wind?

'Cause you just breezed in here on me?

GAIL. No. You can call me Gail like my name.

WALKING MAN. Okay, then.

GAIL. Okay.

WALKING MAN. Who *are* you, though?

GAIL. Who are *you*, though?

WALKING MAN. I live here.

GAIL. You going on a trip?

Looks like you on your way somewhere.

WALKING MAN. I am.

GAIL. Where?

WALKING MAN. Lots of places.

GAIL. *(Pronounced "KAY-Row.")* Cairo?

WALKING MAN. Maybe

GAIL. That's where I'm from. You can skip it, ain't nothin' special there.

WALKING MAN. I ain't skippin' over no place.

GAIL. …

Where you from? I know you ain't from here.

WALKING MAN. Why not?

GAIL. I'm saying *from.*

WALKING MAN. …

GAIL. Where'd you grow up?

Where was you born?

WALKING MAN. Right underneath that tree there.

GAIL. No you wasn't.

WALKING MAN. How you gonna tell me?

GAIL. Who gave birth to you?

WALKING MAN. My mama.

GAIL. What she name you?

WALKING MAN. Walking Man.

GAIL. What kinda name is that?

WALKING MAN. My name.

GAIL. Why is that your name?

WALKING MAN. 'Cause I be walking places. Been walking since the womb. You know how babies be kickin'? I ain't kick. I walked. Stepped.

Came out my mama and was walkin' that same day. Like a baby giraffe.

GAIL. I don't believe that.

WALKING MAN. You don't got to believe it.

GAIL. ...

And now you going to Cairo with a bag and a stick.

WALKING MAN. Not just Cairo. Every place. Every city.

GAIL. Don't see why.

If I had a place like this to live I wouldn't never leave it.

WALKING MAN. How'd you get here?

Where was you headed to?

GAIL. Anywhere but my house.

WALKING MAN. Why?

GAIL. ...

It's flooded. My folks are going up to Future City – and I said, flooding up there is gonna be worse than Cairo, not better.

WALKING MAN. In Cairo they at least got levies. Future City don't have no levies.

GAIL. Right that's what I'm tryna tell them. I said we need to be going East, not north, y'all don't make no sense.

They said, Gail you grown. Go 'head and have your little walk and we'll see you up there in Future when you get hungry. I said, *No you won't.*

They know I'm hardheaded, so, they won't be expecting me for at least a month. I'ma hold out longer if I can.

WALKING MAN. ...

GAIL. What about you, where you tryna go?

WALKING MAN. I got things I need to do.

GAIL. Alright.

At least you packed. Me, I just up and left. I said, you know what, this is it. If I start packing, then I'ma start thinking. And if I start thinking, I might start doubting. And if I start doubting, I might just end up floating down them Future City streets with all these other fools.

WALKING MAN. How'd you end up *here*?

Ain't even no good roads out this way.

GAIL. Well, as soon as I stepped outside my door, I heard the ocean.

Of course it was just the high *river* I was hearin'.

But then I thought, well: it's *going* to the ocean.

You know?

WALKING MAN. ...

GAIL. What *is* it about the ocean?!

WALKING MAN. I don't know.

GAIL. ...

It's undeniable. That's the thing about it. That's the word.

The giant, undeniable ocean.

GAIL. And then there's the little Mississippi. Which we call the mighty Mississippi, right, but who are we kiddin'?

...

The ocean must love the Mississippi so, so much.

Because the Mississippi just rushes into its arms again and again and again.

And it don't never stop.

It can't never give enough.

And that's such a song, ain't it?

So I went outside and I followed it. I waded through the song of the Mississippi. But I think I started following it wrong 'cause then I was on the bank of a smaller river. And then I was following a stream. And it started gettin' dark. And then I saw this light. This light in the forest. And so I go toward it.

And this man and this woman, they meet me and they give me this lighter. And they lead me deeper and deeper into the trees.

And then they're gone.

They gone like shadows.

WALKING MAN. Who do you think they were?

GAIL. I think they were my guardian angels.

WALKING MAN. Why you think that?

GAIL. This lighter is something else.

Hold it.

> (**WALKING MAN** *holds the lighter in his hand.*)

You'd think it'd be heavy, right?

WALKING MAN. …

GAIL. And all you have to do to light it,

You just open up the top there.

That's all.

> *(He does so.)*

Look how high that flame goes.

…

If that's not an angel gift I don't know what is.

> *(**WALKING MAN** offers **GAIL** the pipe.)*

WALKING MAN. *(Re: the pipe.)* Do you want some?

GAIL. Sure.

> *(**WALKING MAN** passes the pipe.)*
>
> *(**GAIL** puffs.)*

I think it's out.

> *(She taps the pipe, loosening the tobacco.)*
>
> *(He lights it for her.)*

So. Am I keeping you?

WALKING MAN. I don't know.

GAIL. Okay.

WALKING MAN. …

You wanna stay up and talk all night?

GAIL. What you wanna talk about?

WALKING MAN. …

Everything.

GAIL. Everything.

...

Okay.

WALKING MAN. Okay.

(They sit down together.)

End of Play

Part 3:
Early's House

PART 3: EARLY'S HOUSE was originally produced in New York City by Roundabout Theatre Company in association with New York Theatre Workshop at the Harold and Miriam Steinberg Center for Theatre / Laura Pels Theatre on October 11, 2023. The performance was directed by Patricia McGregor, with set design by Arnulfo Maldonado, lighting design by Stacey Derosier, costume design by Emilio Sosa, and original music and sound design by Marc Anthony Thompson. The production stage manager was Katie Ailinger. The cast was as follows:

EARLY	Nicole Ari Parker
CRAZY EDDIE	Daniel J. Watts

CHARACTERS

EARLY – (W, 20s) A young woman who has survived the winter.
CRAZY EDDIE – (M, 20s) A young man from a nearby town.

SETTING

A small clearing in a big forest in southern Illinois.

TIME

Spring. The 1950s.

AUTHOR'S NOTES

An ellipsis line in the dialogue [...] represents a pause, a beat or perhaps a physical action.

When a line of dialogue ends in a dash [–] this means the next line comes right on top of it, perhaps with an overlap.

Where an overlap is needed in a specific place, it is marked by a slash [/].

(Night.)

(Starlight shines through a canopy of ancient trees.)

(Under a particularly large tree, **EARLY** *lies awake. Next to her is a bundle of blankets.)*

(She looks up at the tree.)

EARLY. He know if he come up here, he'll shake.

He'll shake so much his skin will fall right off his bones.

I'm the only one these paths are roads for.

Everybody else gets thorns in they feet and mosquitos in they eyes.

He come for me,

And my ears turn into owl ears and I hear his heartbeat a mile off,

And I perch in your branches, and I grow feathers,

And my eyes shine in the dark,

And I look far, far out to him,

And aim into his ear and say

(A terrifyingly loud shriek.)

OOOOOOOOOOOOOOOOOOOOO-EEEE!

...

And I watch him.

Watch him stop right in his tracks.

EARLY. And then I spread my wings, silent, and I soar,

Silent.

Silent, silent, silent –

There ain't no silence like that silence.

The flying owl, that be the silence in the mind of God, I think.

That's *real* silence.

All other silence got to bow down to that silence.

…

You know all about it.

But he don't know.

He don't know a thing 'til I circle him, pass him in silence, pass by his head in silence like a spirit, pass by his left-side first and make him look left, pass by his right side,

And now I'm gone back home.

Back home to you.

And he back there afraid.

He don't wanna be passed on two sides, silent.

He don't wanna fall down into the mud

He don't wanna feed the leeches.

He don't wanna be thin in the swamp.

He don't wanna be bones.

>   *(She looks long and hard at the bundle of blankets beside her.)*

…

Baby?

You awake?

You been woke this whole time?

You can't be listenin' to Mama when she talkin' on like that and not tell her.

You gotta cry! You gotta cry so I know you awake.

> *(Picks up the bundle and cradles it.)*

You gonna have to learn to cry, baby.

> *(Pats the baby. Softly at first, then more forcefully.)*

Come on, just a little cry for Mama. Show me how you gonna cry if you need something.

BABY. *(A very short grunt.) Ah.*

EARLY. That ain't no cry you silly-man!

Silly-man silly-man-silly-man!

BABY. *Ah.*

EARLY. You silly little man!

BABY. *AH!*

EARLY. You talkin' to your mama? You talkin' to your wild mama Queen of the Forest?

What you got to say to the Queen of the Forest?

BABY. *Ah.*

EARLY. *Ah.*

BABY. *Ah-ah.*

EARLY. You hungry?

BABY. *Ah.*

EARLY. Look at you. With your little walking legs and you can't even *cry*.

You gonna walk before you cry?

> (**EARLY** *nurses the baby.*)

You babyman.

You walking legs babyman. Need to go to sleep. Gotta go down to the river again in the morning.

Need some more water.

We outa meat, we gonna have to catch us some fish.

…

You need to go to sleep, okay?

…

You gonna sleep?

…

Mama needs to sleep. Mama's sleepy.

…

…

You 'sleep?

BABY. *Ah.*

EARLY. *Ah.*

Ah yourself you baby walking man.

> (*The sound of an engine, distant at first, then closer.*)
>
> (*Headlights shine in* **EARLY**'s *face.*)
>
> (*A rusty, gray pickup truck enters.*)
>
> (*Driving the pickup truck is* **CRAZY EDDIE**.)

> (**EARLY** *closes her eyes and leans against the tree, as if to somehow camouflage herself against it.*)
>
> (**CRAZY EDDIE** *leans out the window to get a better look at* **EARLY**.)
>
> (*He turns off the engine and opens the door.*)

CRAZY EDDIE. Early!?

...

Did I find you?

That you, Early?

> (*He turns the headlights off and gets out of the truck, holding an electric lantern.*)
>
> (*He walks to* **EARLY**.)
>
> (*He has a very pronounced limp.*)

Early?

EARLY. No.

CRAZY EDDIE. That ain't you?

EARLY. No.

CRAZY EDDIE. You sure?

EARLY. Yes.

CRAZY EDDIE. That's you!

EARLY. ...

Edward?

CRAZY EDDIE. Who you hiding from?

EARLY. ...

CRAZY EDDIE. I go by Crazy Eddie now. Ain't you heard? Don't know if word got around to you. Thought it would. Yeah I'm Crazy Eddie.

You can still call me Edward. Or Ed. Or just Eddie.

Eduapolis.

Whatever feel right to you, that's fine. I got a lot of names that fit me.

EARLY. ...

CRAZY EDDIE. How long you been out here?

EARLY. ...

CRAZY EDDIE. Well hey, I'm glad I found you.

...

What you out here hiding from, Early?

EARLY. ...

CRAZY EDDIE. You don't give no clues, do you?

You got a face like a statue playin' poker.

You don't give *no* clues.

EARLY. ...

CRAZY EDDIE. You hungry?

I brought a lot of food.

A whole grocery aisle's worth of food. What you hungry for?

EARLY. ...

CRAZY EDDIE. You can't even say what you hungry for?

EARLY. ...

Don't need no food from you, I can get my own.

CRAZY EDDIE. Candy bar?

EARLY. No.

CRAZY EDDIE. Licorice?

EARLY. No.

CRAZY EDDIE. Bread?

EARLY. No.

CRAZY EDDIE. Budweiser?

EARLY. No.

CRAZY EDDIE. I got about a six-pack and a half in there.

EARLY. No.

CRAZY EDDIE. Ham sandwich?

EARLY. No.

CRAZY EDDIE. Ice cream?

EARLY. No.

CRAZY EDDIE. Might as well, it's gonna melt.

EARLY. No.

CRAZY EDDIE. Orange juice.

EARLY. No.

CRAZY EDDIE. Cranberry juice.

EARLY. No.

CRAZY EDDIE. Meatloaf? I got a meatloaf in there. It's already cooked.

EARLY. No.

CRAZY EDDIE. Rock candy?

EARLY. No.

CRAZY EDDIE. Cheese? I got a block of cheese or two in there.

EARLY. Stop asking.

CRAZY EDDIE. ...

Coca-Cola?

EARLY. Stop asking me.

CRAZY EDDIE. I can mix the Coca-Cola and the Budweiser together.

EARLY. ...

CRAZY EDDIE. I can mix the orange juice and the cranberry juice together.

EARLY. ...

CRAZY EDDIE. I can put some cheese in an ice-cream cone.

EARLY. ...

CRAZY EDDIE. That's actually good.

> (**EARLY** *picks up a hammer.* **CRAZY EDDIE** *moves away from her.*)

WHOA!

...

...

You *is* you!

That hammer? That's Early.

EARLY. You don't know the first thing about this hammer.

CRAZY EDDIE. First time I ever saw you, you was killing something with that thing.

EARLY. ...

You don't know what you talking about.

CRAZY EDDIE. You couldn't have been more than three years old. It was a rabbit you was killin', I think. In the front yard of your house? I was walking by with my friends –

EARLY. Don't know why you be spying on kids in they yards –

CRAZY EDDIE. I was a kid, too, / what you mean –

EARLY. With your good-for-nothing friends –

CRAZY EDDIE. We wasn't spying on nobody we was passing by –

EARLY. Okay, then, pass by. You can go. I didn't ask you to run after me, Edward. Crazy Eddie. Whoever you is.

> (**CRAZY EDDIE** *limps back to the truck.*)
>
> (*He gets into the truck. He turns the ignition. The headlights come on, but the truck will not start.*)
>
> (**CRAZY EDDIE** *waits a moment.*)
>
> (*He tries again. The engine won't turn over.*)
>
> (**CRAZY EDDIE** *sits for another moment.*)
>
> (*He leans partially out of the window to speak to* **EARLY**.)

CRAZY EDDIE. I just put a new engine in. Shouldn't be no problems.

I'll let it rest for a minute and I'll try again, alright?

EARLY. ...

CRAZY EDDIE. You sure you don't want nothing to eat?

EARLY. ...

CRAZY EDDIE. I'll get these lights outa your face.

> (**CRAZY EDDIE** *turns off the headlights.*)

...

CRAZY EDDIE. There's a lot of spirits out here.

I think they got into the engine.

Them spirits, 'ey,

Sometimes they play with you.

They be playin' games with us sometime just 'cause they got nothin' better to do.

EARLY. ...

CRAZY EDDIE. I'll try it again.

>   (**CRAZY EDDIE** *tries again.*)

>   (*The headlights brighten intensely, then fizzle out. The engine is still dead.*)

Whoa! You see that?

EARLY. Stay where you are.

CRAZY EDDIE. You saw that didn't you?

You saw how bright my lights got.

EARLY. You got it right up in my eyes.

CRAZY EDDIE. I ain't try to blind you or nothing.

I was tryna do what you asked me to and drive away.

>   (**CRAZY EDDIE** *opens the door to his truck and gets out.*)

EARLY. Stay in your truck!

>   (**CRAZY EDDIE** *gets back in his truck.*)

Close the door.

>   (**CRAZY EDDIE** *closes the door.*)

>   (*He sits in the truck.*)

(He leans his head out the window.)

CRAZY EDDIE. Ey, do this for me right quick –

EARLY. I ain't doin' nothin' for you leave me alone –

CRAZY EDDIE. Alright, but just do this, though –

EARLY. It's like you can't hear me when I say no I ain't doin' nothing for you.

CRAZY EDDIE. Okay.

Okay.

I hear you.

…

All I'll say is, if a person were to leave her head still and move her eyes all the way to the right, and then real quick move 'em to the left,

She'd see spirits.

That's all I'm sayin'.

I ain't askin' you to do nothin' for me. Okay?

EARLY. …

CRAZY EDDIE. You don't gotta do nothing on account of me.

EARLY. …

…

…

CRAZY EDDIE. Did you do it?

EARLY. Yes.

CRAZY EDDIE. You see anything?

EARLY. I saw flashing light. 'Cause I'm half blind.

CRAZY EDDIE. Right. That's the spirits. That light? That's them spirits dancing.

EARLY. That's light.

CRAZY EDDIE. Can you see flashes around the car?

EARLY. ...

Yes

CRAZY EDDIE. See. They still hovering around. They still messin' with us. Let me test somethin'.

> *(He turns the key in the ignition. Nothing happens at all.)*

See! Look at this: when I turn the ignition: have you ever seen anything like that in your life!? I turn the ignition and don't nothin' happen. No turnover. No click. No headlights.

This thing might as well be a rock.

Them spirits might not be just playin' around.

They might be upset.

EARLY. ...

CRAZY EDDIE. If I stay in my truck.

If I stay right here in the truck, can I stay here?

Soon as it gets light out I'll walk up to the road. I promise.

EARLY. Don't be talkin' to me.

CRAZY EDDIE. Alright.

EARLY. At all.

> *(**CRAZY EDDIE** gives a thumbs up and rolls up his window.)*
>
> *(They sit in silence for a long, long, long time.)*

(**CRAZY EDDIE** *opens a bag of chips.*)

(*He eats chips.*)

(**EARLY** *rocks her baby.*)

(...)

(*She sees or somehow senses the chips.*)

(*She walks to the truck and knocks on the window.*)

(**CRAZY EDDIE** *rolls the window down.*)

(**EARLY** *reaches in and grabs the bag of chips.*)

(*She goes back to her place by the tree.*)

(*She eats chips.*)

(**CRAZY EDDIE** *finds an apple and begins eating it. But he obviously wants the chips.*)

(*They both eat.*)

(*They eat.*)

(*They eat.*)

(**CRAZY EDDIE** *leans his head out the window.*)

I know you ain't gonna ask me for these chips.

CRAZY EDDIE. I just wanted a few more.

EARLY. I give you a place to sleep and you can't even share a bag of chips!?

CRAZY EDDIE. I'm okay with sharin 'em I just want some, too.

...

EARLY. You ain't say you had no potato chips. I love potato chips.

Why you try to hide the potato chips?

CRAZY EDDIE. I ain't hide nothing. I asked you if you wanted them and you said no.

EARLY. No I didn't.

CRAZY EDDIE. Yes you did.

EARLY. I did not say no to no chips.

CRAZY EDDIE. You said no to everything.

EARLY. You didn't say chips.

CRAZY EDDIE. 'Cause I gave up.

EARLY. You shoulda said chips first.

CRAZY EDDIE. ...

EARLY. How you gonna not say it and then it's the first thing you eat?

CRAZY EDDIE. ...

Did I say crisps instead of chips? Sometimes I say crisps without thinkin' about it.

EARLY. What's that?

CRAZY EDDIE. That's what they be callin' 'em over the pond.

EARLY. Which pond?

CRAZY EDDIE. The big pond. The big one.

EARLY. The pond over behind the train station? Ain't nobody live across that pond.

CRAZY EDDIE. No, the ocean.

EARLY. Why you didn't say ocean then if you meant ocean?

CRAZY EDDIE. 'Cause you can call it a pond once you been across it. And I been across it.

EARLY. Well you shoulda gotten more crisps while you was over there 'cause these mine. And I ain't giving you no more, you already ate half the bag.

>(**EARLY** *eats.*)

>(**CRAZY EDDIE** *begins to roll up the window of the truck.*)

You can leave the window down if you want to.

>(**CRAZY EDDIE** *leaves the window down.*)

What other food you got in there?

CRAZY EDDIE. Like I said: Some jerky. Some apples. Got me some rock candy. Got some peanuts. Got some big jugs of water. Got some flour. Got some peanut butter –

EARLY. And you brought all that food for what?

CRAZY EDDIE. For you.

For us.

If you wanted to share.

EARLY. ...

...

>(**EARLY** *goes to the truck.*)

Can I have some water?

>(**CRAZY EDDIE** *passes a large jug of water to* **EARLY**.)

CRAZY EDDIE. Got some cups if you need one.

>(**EARLY** *returns to her spot.*)

(**EARLY** *lifts the jug and drinks from it.*)

EARLY. Why don't you walk right?

CRAZY EDDIE. I do walk right. Just can't walk *fast*.

EARLY. You walk like a monster.

CRAZY EDDIE. Says who?

EARLY. Says the way you walk.

CRAZY EDDIE. I got me a slow walk, so what?

EARLY. …

…

I'll take a cup please.

CRAZY EDDIE. …

It's okay with you if I get out of the truck?

EARLY. To bring me the cup, yes.

CRAZY EDDIE. Then I gotta come back in here?

EARLY. Yes.

CRAZY EDDIE. …

(**CRAZY EDDIE** *brings* **EARLY** *a cup.*)

EARLY. See, that's a monster walk.

CRAZY EDDIE. No it ain't. This how I strut.

EARLY. Your strut is *broke*.

CRAZY EDDIE. My strut can't be broke.

EARLY. What is it then?

CRAZY EDDIE. It's mine.

I start walkin' like someone else: that's when the strut is broke.

EARLY. Alright then, strut yourself back up in that truck.

CRAZY EDDIE. I'm on my way.

(**CRAZY EDDIE** *walks back to the truck.*)

EARLY. For real, why you walk like that?

...

What's wrong with your legs?

CRAZY EDDIE. Nothin'. That's the way they is now.

EARLY. ...

CRAZY EDDIE. They got bullets in 'em.

EARLY. ...

...

You tellin' me a story?

CRAZY EDDIE. I ain't.

EARLY. Yes you is. How many bullets?

CRAZY EDDIE. Eight.

EARLY. That's a story.

CRAZY EDDIE. ...

EARLY. Eight?

CRAZY EDDIE. ...

EARLY. You ain't got no eight bullets.

Where you get 'em from? Who shot you eight times in the legs?

CRAZY EDDIE. I have no idea.

It was a lotta people runnin' around and they was all wearing the same outfits.

EARLY. What you talkin' about?

CRAZY EDDIE. The war.

EARLY. See. Now I *know* you tellin' stories. I seen you after you got back from the war. I seen you at the store.

You wasn't walkin' like that.

CRAZY EDDIE. If you was lookin' at me you woulda seen it.

If you was really lookin', and you saw me walkin', you woulda seen it.

You ain't never really looked at me before, that's all.

EARLY. ...

...

You got eight war bullets up in your legs.

CRAZY EDDIE. Yes ma'am.

EARLY. They still there.

CRAZY EDDIE. Yes they are.

EARLY. But the war's over.

CRAZY EDDIE. So they say.

EARLY. The war's *been* over.

CRAZY EDDIE. That's what they sayin'.

EARLY. Why the bullets still in there?

CRAZY EDDIE. Oh, you know how bullets be.

Bullets, boy, bullets like to stay where they at once they get there.

EARLY. Is that what they told you at the hospital?

They didn't try to remove them?

CRAZY EDDIE. What hospital?

EARLY. Thought if you got shot up at the war they take you to the hospital.

CRAZY EDDIE. Ain't no hospitals in wars.

We all there to kill each other.

EARLY. But they don't take you to a tent? Like in the movies? There's soldiers and there's nurses taking care of 'em?

CRAZY EDDIE. Oh, you mean the *field* hospital.

Yeah, them field hospitals, boy.

It ain't like no hospital in them field hospitals. And it ain't like the movies either.

In them field hospitals – 'ey, them field hospitals are somethin' else. Them field hospitals, first off they don't smell right. Second off, they don't sound right.

People getting arms and legs taken off, sometime.

People comin' in and they don't have but half a head.

People cryin' and talkin' to themselves.

It ain't right, but it *is* though.

You look around and you know it ain't right.

But it is what it is and everybody know that too.

Everybody know not to say nothin' if some grown man cryin'.

You can talk to anybody.

You can say whatever you want to anybody that meet your eye.

Sometime you wake up in the middle of the night and the man next to you lookin' at you. And he might be alive, he might be dead. You can look back or not.

Ain't like no movie up in there. Movies make sense.

In movies there's some sense in everything. Them field hospitals don't make no sense.

EARLY. Why didn't they take out your bullets?

CRAZY EDDIE. They tried to.

But I said you know what? I'll keep my bullets.

What if I get home and they try to say I didn't fight?

They did that to Earl.

'Member Big Earl?

He had to go build him a place by the tracks, out there in Future City. Had to build him one of them shacks. They took his arms off after he got shot up, and he thought he could get a house out of it.

They supposed to help him buy a house if he want it. And if they wasn't gonna do that, he knew they'd at least give him a pension, and he'd use that for his house.

But they try to say he wasn't even there.

Tried to say he didn't fight.

He said, I'm Big Earl.

They said, We don't know that.

He said, I fought. Look at me. I got no arms. And I got papers for proof if you need 'em.

You know what they say to Big Earl?

They say: We need your fingerprints.

…

How wrong is that?

Looked an armless soldier dead in his eye and said: we need your fingerprints.

Big Earl was so mad, he went by the tracks in Future City where all them houses and shacks be at

And built himself his own shack.

Was so mad he built a shack even though he didn't have no arms.

I don't know how he did that, but he *did it*.

That's where he stay now.

So I got wind of that and I said no y'all not takin these bullets. These my proof.

And they know I got my proof.

But I ain't takin' no money from them.

These bullets gainin' interest. 'Til they pay big Earl.

EARLY. ...

...

>   (**EARLY** *walks to the truck.*)

Can I have a piece of rock candy?

>   (**CRAZY EDDIE** *gives* **EARLY** *a piece of rock candy.*)
>
>   (**EARLY** *walks back to her spot with the candy.*)
>
>   *(She pops it in her mouth.)*

You want a piece?

CRAZY EDDIE. I got a piece.

EARLY. You eatin' it right now?

CRAZY EDDIE. Yeah.

EARLY. Come over here and eat it next to me.

>   (**CRAZY EDDIE** *gets out of the truck.*)

Bring your light.

>   (**CRAZY EDDIE** *grabs his lantern and walks to* **EARLY.** *He sits.*)

(They eat rock candy and don't say anything for a moment.)

(...)

EARLY. I forgot how much I like rock candy.

CRAZY EDDIE. Good, ain't it?

EARLY. I like how you can't eat it fast.

I like how it's sweet but you can't eat it fast even if you want to.

CRAZY EDDIE. ...

...

You been out here since when?

EARLY. November.

CRAZY EDDIE. ...

You ain't. There ain't no way.

Hey. Hey, there ain't no way you been here since November. That's too long. 'Ey, if you was here since November, the animals woulda had a fight over who gets to eat you first.

EARLY. I *have* been here since November.

CRAZY EDDIE. How'd you make it through the winter?

EARLY. I hibernated.

CRAZY EDDIE. You hibernated?

'Ey, you can't just up and decide to hibernate one day.

That ain't no easy thing to do.

EARLY. I know it ain't.

CRAZY EDDIE. How'd you do it, then?

EARLY. I cheated.

CRAZY EDDIE. Oh, okay. That's smart.

How'd you cheat?

EARLY. ...

CRAZY EDDIE. If it's okay to tell me.

Maybe you don't want me to know.

EARLY. I can tell you.

...

I found this spot in November. The sky was clear most every day and the sunlight kept it warm. But at nighttime, this little man here, I felt his fingers getting cold –

CRAZY EDDIE. Man? A tiny man? Where he at?

EARLY. My *baby*.

CRAZY EDDIE. Baby?

...

There's a baby in them blankets?

EARLY. Of course there is, what you thought?

CRAZY EDDIE. I thought you was holdin' blankets.

EARLY. Why would I hold the blankets in my arms like this if there wasn't no baby?

CRAZY EDDIE. Hey, people be doin' all type of things.

EARLY. You thought I was a crazy or somethin'?

CRAZY EDDIE. Hey I'm Crazy Eddie. Crazy ain't crazy to me.

You know what's crazy?

People not bein' crazy. That shit is crazy.

How you gonna sit there and not be crazy when crazy happenin' all over the place?

EARLY. ...

CRAZY EDDIE. I can't even keep up with everyone's crazy anymore.

My little brother? 'Ey, he ten times crazier than me. At least.

EARLY. Who you talkin' about, little Dax?

What'd little Dax say when you left with all this food in your truck?

CRAZY EDDIE. He ain't see me leave.

...

Nobody did.

EARLY. ...

CRAZY EDDIE. I'm gonna grab me another apple. You want one?

EARLY. No thank you, Edward.

CRAZY EDDIE. You for sure? Apple go good with them chips if you got some chips left. You sure?

EARLY. I'm sure.

CRAZY EDDIE. You don't like no salt on your apples, huh?

EARLY. I don't want no apples, that's all.

CRAZY EDDIE. Oh, okay. You don't want none. You don't feel like no apples right now. Alright.

EARLY. Edward. Why you always makin'... why you always...

CRAZY EDDIE. Why I what?

EARLY. I don't know. Never mind.

CRAZY EDDIE. I apologize.

EARLY. ...

...

You want me to tell you how I hibernated or not?

CRAZY EDDIE. Yeah, how'd you do it? How'd you cheat your way through it?

EARLY. So like I said, my little baby's fingers are feelin' cold / and I'm –

CRAZY EDDIE. Wait, wait, wait, wait, wait, / wait a minute –

EARLY. What!

CRAZY EDDIE. Where'd the baby come from? I wanna know that first.

EARLY. ...

The baby came from the river.

CRAZY EDDIE. No, I want the real story.

EARLY. That is the real story.

CRAZY EDDIE. Babies don't come from rivers, they come from jai-jais.

EARLY. What?

CRAZY EDDIE. The baby ain't come from your jai-jai?

EARLY. ...

Jai-jai?

CRAZY EDDIE. That's what my mama call 'em.

EARLY. Don't ever say that again, please.

CRAZY EDDIE. Okay.

EARLY. The baby came from the river.

CRAZY EDDIE. Like Moses.

EARLY. ...

Yes.

CRAZY EDDIE. *(Takes a quick look at the baby.)* Nope.

That's a jai-jai baby. That's a regular old baby that ain't no Moses.

EARLY. Well he's Moses to me.

CRAZY EDDIE. That what his name is? That's little Moses?

EARLY. I don't know.

CRAZY EDDIE. How you don't know what you named him?

EARLY. I don't know what I named him 'cause I ain't named him yet.

CRAZY EDDIE. That baby is huuuuuge!

How you ain't named him!? You gonna get that child in some trouble! How old is he?

EARLY. Just six months.

CRAZY EDDIE. *Just* six months?! *Just.*

And you ain't named him yet?

And you tryna name him *Moses*?

EARLY. Maybe. I like Moses.

CRAZY EDDIE. You name your baby Moses and the real Moses gonna hear. You name your baby Moses, he'll have to part a sea.

You think he can do that?

EARLY. If he needs to.

CRAZY EDDIE. He looks kinda funny, don't he?

EARLY. That's what I looked like when I was a baby.

CRAZY EDDIE. Of course, 'cause he came out your jai-jai.

EARLY. ...

...

    (**EARLY** *lets out a deafening screech.*)

OOOOOOOOOOOOOOOOOOOOOOOOOOOO-EEEE!!!!

(**CRAZY EDDIE** *is rocked back by the sound.*)

(**EARLY** *stares him down.*)

CRAZY EDDIE. I'll never say it again.

I promise.

EARLY. ...

I killed a bear.

CRAZY EDDIE. ...

Say what?

EARLY. My baby's fingers was getting cold. And I couldn't keep 'em warm. And I thought, Where am I gonna go? Can't go back home. This my home now.

This is the place that gave me shelter when I ain't have shelter.

This the place that gave me a bed of leaves to sleep on when I needed just a bit of softness.

This the place my little walking-man was born.

This the earth that know my blood

And my pain.

This the earth that know my name.

Not Kay-Ro. Not Future City. Not Culver City. Not Carbondale. Not Springfield. *Not* Tennessee. *Not* Chicago. *Not* New York. *Not* Egypt. *Not* Jerusalem.

This is the place

That knows who I am.

And I ain't leavin it.

...

...

EARLY. But my baby's fingers. They cold.

So I think to myself. Who survives out here in winter without no house?

The Bear. The Bear do that.

Now my grandma she tell me there's bears deep in these forests. But you won't never find them. 'Cause they make themselves into shadows and they don't like to be seen. But she say they there. They always been there, and they still is, she say.

And now I know I need to find me one.

So I climb up that tree. And I look. And I listen.

For a whole day I look and I listen.

And yes, I hear one.

And then I see him.

He scratching at the trees, diggin in the ground. I reckon he tryna fatten up. And he must have a place where he gonna go to rest.

So I climb down. And I strap my little man to my back. And I go off and I track that bear. I find where he's walked. I find where he's eaten. I find where he's left his scent. And I follow,

And I follow,

And I follow.

With my baby on my back, with my hammer, I follow,

And I see where his tracks lead. Into his little den.

So I wait outside that den. And when all the stars is out I put my ear near the hole and I hear him breathin'.

And I can feel my little man on my back. He breathing like that, too. His head is resting against my back and he's dreaming.

And I get down low.

And I whisper a prayer to the screech owl. I ask the owl if I can borrow her silence.

And I crawl in.

And it's dark as the end of the world in there, but I can feel it in the air where he is.

And I swing my hammer hard as I can. Right down on his head. And I feel him start to move. And I swing again.

And I swing again.

And I feel the skull give way.

And he stops moving.

And he stops breathing.

And I have my place to sleep.

And I make me a fire just outside. And I have meat. And bones.

And it snowed that night. It snowed and snowed and snowed and snowed. Buried the meat as deep as I could in that fresh snow. Prayed to God the cold would stay. It did.

The meat lasted. The bones lasted.

...

And me and baby walky-walk, we slept most of the winter right there. Woke up and ate.

Snow for water, bear for food. Went to sleep again.

...

That's how I hibernated.

That's how I cheated.

CRAZY EDDIE. ...

...

You don't supposed to kill bears.

EARLY. ...

CRAZY EDDIE. I mean good *job*.

But that's bad luck.

Killing bears. Makin' your baby walk around without a name.

Lord have mercy.

EARLY. ...

You really think so?

CRAZY EDDIE. You can't kill a bear and get away with it.

EARLY. Why?

CRAZY EDDIE. Around here?

EARLY. Why not?

CRAZY EDDIE. Them bears? Them bears don't *play*. Bears they take themselves real serious. You kill 'em and they don't like it.

...

You got any of the bones left?

EARLY. I got the skull.

CRAZY EDDIE. You kept the skull?!

EARLY. You wanna see it?

(**EARLY** *presents a badly damaged bear skull.*)

CRAZY EDDIE. ...

...

Sweet God. Look at that.

You really did knock his brains out.

> (**CRAZY EDDIE** *takes the skull to his truck.*)
>
> (*He looks at the skull.*)
>
> (*Looks at the truck.*)

EARLY. What you doin?

CRAZY EDDIE. It's that Bear spirit, probably, that messed up the truck.

EARLY. Why you think it was the bear?

CRAZY EDDIE. That truck was runnin' great 'til tonight.

EARLY. That truck is old and rusty.

CRAZY EDDIE. But it run just fine. I put in a whole new engine just last month. That thing ain't never shut down on me. And now it's shut down.

> (**CRAZY EDDIE** *carefully places the skull on the hood of the truck.*)

EARLY. …

CRAZY EDDIE. And what it do when it shut down: remember? Lit up like crazy. Lit up right in your eyes. Lord have mercy, I thought someone was maybe foolin' around with you, but you got a bear spirit that ain't happy. You got a bear spirit angry at you.

EARLY. I ain't even think about that.

CRAZY EDDIE. Good job, by the way. Did I tell you that? Good job.

EARLY. Yes.

You told me that.

CRAZY EDDIE. You know, I ain't never talked to you this long?

Well I guess you do know.

We ain't never talked this long, you and I.

You good to talk to, Early.

You good to have for company.

EARLY. That why you came out here? For the company?

CRAZY EDDIE. Well, you know I quit my job and I thought I should come find you if I could. Since I had this truck and all this food I took from the grocery. I can't just sit at home with it.

EARLY. Why'd you quit your job?

CRAZY EDDIE. I guess I thought if I could find you you'd probably need something to eat and drink.

And I guess I thought since I work at the grocery anyway I should just take some food and drinks from there.

But to the store, you know, that ain't *food* I'm taking. That's *inventory*. And if I take inventory out of the store, they probably ain't gonna want me to come back. So I ain't come back. I went out. Took all the money out of my savings account, put it all in some envelopes in case I need it. And I took it all with me. The money and the food.

And I went out and I looked for you.

EARLY. ...

Why'd you look for me?

CRAZY EDDIE. Everyone at your house, and all your neighbors, all they said was you *left*.

That didn't add up to me.

I did some asking around. I asked people, I said, Is there any place, or anybody Early was tryna get to? And they ain't say.

And I said, Is there anybody Early was tryna leave away from?

And that ain't say nothing. But that nothing was a little louder than the first nothing. And so I asked about that.

I said, what's goin' on with this loudass nothin' you sayin'?

And folks was sayin', you know / they was sayin' you –

EARLY. Why'd you want to find me though, Edward?

You and I ain't never spent no time together.

CRAZY EDDIE. I can't say why I do half the things I do. I noticed you wasn't around. I thought, where's Early gotten off to?

And after a while, well...

I got to missing you for some reason.

Don't make no sense.

But I stopped tryna do that a few years ago. Stopped tryna make sense. I said if I'm missin' Early there must be a reason. And knowin' there is a reason,

That's more important sometimes than knowing what the reason is. You know what I mean?

EARLY. You mean like how flowers know it's Spring even though they don't have no calendar?

CRAZY EDDIE. ...

Right.

Exactly like that.

EARLY. ...

CRAZY EDDIE. It's nice to be understood.

...

Maybe that's why I missed you.

Maybe I knew you'd understand me even when I didn't really know what I was talkin' about.

'Cause the truth is I only *kinda* know what I'm talkin' about most of the time.

It don't stop me from talkin'. But some people don't like that.

EARLY. When I heard you went off to the war I remember thinking,

I wonder if Edward will ever make it back? Probably not.

But then there you were again in the grocery store one day

And I thought, How is he the *same*?

War is supposed to change people. And he's the same. He's the same goofy boy in the store that he always was. How did *that* happen?

CRAZY EDDIE. ...

I ain't the same.

I'm good at makin' it seem like I am.

EARLY. ...

CRAZY EDDIE. Can I ask you something, Early?

Will you tell the truth if I ask you something?

EARLY. ...

I think so.

CRAZY EDDIE. Whose baby is that?

Besides yours?

EARLY. ...

CRAZY EDDIE. Who sent you out here like this?

EARLY. ...

...

I'm never going to say.

CRAZY EDDIE. ...

Okay.

You don't have to say.

He looks just like you anyway.

EARLY. ...

CRAZY EDDIE. He looks like the river, too.

EARLY. ...

...

Did you really miss me?

CRAZY EDDIE. I did.

EARLY. Do you really think I understand you?

CRAZY EDDIE. Yes. You do understand me.

EARLY. ...

Can I look at your legs?

CRAZY EDDIE. ...

EARLY. You lied, didn't you?

CRAZY EDDIE. I did not lie.

EARLY. ...

...

CRAZY EDDIE. I'm tellin' you the truth.

I try my damnest not to see my legs myself.

If I look at 'em I'm afraid they might up and fall off.

EARLY. Then let *me* see.

Let me see and you don't have to look.

> (**CRAZY EDDIE** *covers his eyes.*)

CRAZY EDDIE. Alright.

> (**EARLY** *begins pulling* **CRAZY EDDIE**'s *pants down.*)
>
> (*It's very tender and very awkward.*)
>
> (...)
>
> (...)

EARLY. ...

Edward...

CRAZY EDDIE. Don't tell me nothin'.

EARLY. Edward, this don't look good.

CRAZY EDDIE. I said don't say nothin'.

Don't tell me things like that.

EARLY. ...

CRAZY EDDIE. Will you pull my pants up now?

EARLY. I'm sorry.

> (**EARLY** *pulls* **CRAZY EDDIE**'s *pants up.*)
>
> (*It's tender, awkward, and painful.*)
>
> (*When she gets the pants up to his knees...*)

CRAZY EDDIE. Okay, I got it from here.

    (**CRAZY EDDIE** *finishes the job.*)

EARLY. Thank you for showing me.

CRAZY EDDIE. ...

Thank you for checking on me.

EARLY. ...

    (**EARLY** *kisses* **CRAZY EDDIE** *on the cheek.*)

    (**CRAZY EDDIE** *kisses* **EARLY** *on the cheek.*)

    (**EARLY** *kisses* **CRAZY EDDIE** *on the other cheek.*)

    (**CRAZY EDDIE** *kisses* **EARLY** *on the other cheek.*)

    (**EARLY** *kisses* **CRAZY EDDIE** *on the lips.*)

    (**CRAZY EDDIE** *kisses her back.*)

    (...)

    (...)

    (**EARLY** *pulls away.*)

CRAZY EDDIE. What I do?

EARLY. ...

CRAZY EDDIE. ...

EARLY. ...

You missed me.

CRAZY EDDIE. I did.

EARLY. Why didn't anybody else miss me?

CRAZY EDDIE. People did miss you.

EARLY. But nobody came to look for me.

...

You didn't even come for six whole months.

CRAZY EDDIE. ...

EARLY. I gave birth to this baby right there.

I gave birth.

Alone.

I caught him myself.

And no one was here.

And no one was on their way.

CRAZY EDDIE. ...

Sorry I was so late.

EARLY. ...

...

CRAZY EDDIE. As soon as I had that first thought "where's Early gotten off to," that's when I shoulda been on my way. That was the first sign and I ain't recognize it. If I had started looking *then* I might have been here when you really needed someone.

Wasn't 'til I got to missin' you. I *had* to do somethin' about that.

So I guess I wasn't really lookin' for you.

I guess in a way I was lookin' for me.

Guess really I was runnin' away too. Took all that food. Took all the money I had saved up from my bank account. And from under my bed.

Told myself I was comin' out to help you.

...

I really *was* thinkin' about you with the food, though.

I ain't know what you would like or what you would need so I just brought a little bit of everything.

Even cooked up a meatloaf before I left. It's cold by now. But it's cooked.

Matterafact I mighta left the oven on.

Oh well.

EARLY. Oh well.

CRAZY EDDIE. ...

It's too late, huh?

Too late for me to really help you.

EARLY. ...

Well,

...

I got just one thing I need to do this spring.

And summer.

One thing to do however many seasons it takes.

CRAZY EDDIE. What's that?

EARLY. Well actually two things.

CRAZY EDDIE. What two things?

EARLY. Three things.

CRAZY EDDIE. What are they?

EARLY. Keep my baby alive.

CRAZY EDDIE. Uhuh.

EARLY. Keep *me* alive.

CRAZY EDDIE. Uhuh.

EARLY. And build me a real place to live. Four walls and a roof.

Maybe even a floor.

CRAZY EDDIE. ...

EARLY. Right here. I don't care if it's gotta be a shack, I don't care if it's a hut, I don't care if it has a million bugs. It's gonna be *here*.

CRAZY EDDIE. ...

EARLY. Will you help me build a house?

CRAZY EDDIE. ...

Sure thing.

EARLY. ...

CRAZY EDDIE. What you wanna build it out of?

EARLY. Whatever we can get.

CRAZY EDDIE. Well you don't wanna go back into town for no supplies...

EARLY. No.

CRAZY EDDIE. And I don't want to either.

EARLY. No, we can't go to town.

CRAZY EDDIE. We could go up to Edwardsville. My name's Edward, so Edwardsville usually treats me okay. Like I said, I got cash. It's all in the glove box there. We can get some lumber.

EARLY. Alright.

...

...

You sure you wanna stay here?

...

You sure you wanna build a house with me?

CRAZY EDDIE. ...

You sure you want me to stay?

> (**EARLY** *approaches* **CRAZY EDDIE.**)

> (*They kiss. It's alright. It's fine.* **EARLY** *lets the kiss in and keeps on breathing.*)

EARLY. ...

Your truck.

The truck don't work.

CRAZY EDDIE. ...

You gotta say somethin to that Bear.

> (**EARLY** *picks up the baby and gets into the passenger side of the truck.*)

> (**CRAZY EDDIE** *gets into the driver's side, picking up the bear skull from the hood.*)

You should drive it, I think.

You the one killed the bear, you need to turn it on.

> (**EARLY** *and* **CRAZY EDDIE** *get out of the truck...*)

> (*And switch places.*)

> (**CRAZY EDDIE** *puts his hand on the skull.*)

> (**EARLY** *prepares to crank the ignition.*)

EARLY. Dear God, bless this bear.

Dear bear, bless us.

And thank you both. Thank you God and thank you bear,

For getting me through the winter. All I had was y'all. And I got through.

And my baby is alive.

And I'm here.

And please...

Please stick with me.

And keep getting me through.

And help Edward with his legs. Help him keep them.

And if he can't keep them, help him let them go. But help him.

And help him to keep being his goofy self.

Help him and protect him. And bless him. And bless me. And bless us.

And thank you.

Thank you, thank you.

*(***EARLY** *turns the key in the ignition.)*

(The truck starts as if it were brand new.)

CRAZY EDDIE. It sound like it's brand new!

With a sound like that it should look brand new. The rust don't look right anymore.

Maybe we can pick up a new coat of paint for it.

EARLY. You got enough money for that?

CRAZY EDDIE. Paint ain't too expensive. It's the cost of the labor they get you on.

I'll paint it myself.

EARLY. Baby walk-walk, what you say? What color we should paint it?

BABY. *Ha-ah.*

EARLY. *Ha-ah.*

CRAZY EDDIE. *Ha-ah. Ha-ah.*

He really talkin' to you, ain't he?

BABY. *Ah-ah-ah.*

EARLY. ...

Okay, so, uh.

Wood. Paint

How much money you got?

> (**CRAZY EDDIE** *opens the glove box and hands an envelope to* **EARLY**.)

It's your money. Just say how much you got.

CRAZY EDDIE. It's our money.

> (**EARLY** *takes out a few bills.*)

EARLY. ...

...

Some nets for fishing

> (*Counts out a few more.*)

Here's for some more chips.

...

Here's for some wood. How much wood we need?

CRAZY EDDIE. To start out? …I'd say set aside…there we go.

EARLY. That's enough?

CRAZY EDDIE. Maybe just a little more.

EARLY. That good?

CRAZY EDDIE. That's good. Yeah.

EARLY. Some summer clothes for little walky-talky man.

What size you think he'll be?

CRAZY EDDIE. Don't know.

EARLY. …

What are we doing?

CRAZY EDDIE. …

Don't know.

EARLY. …

You don't know?

CRAZY EDDIE. …

EARLY. But it's okay, right?

It's okay that we don't know?

>*(**EARLY** looks at **CRAZY EDDIE**.)*
>
>*(She looks.)*
>
>*(She looks.)*
>
>*(…)*
>
>*(She hands the baby to him.)*
>
>*(…)*

*(**CRAZY EDDIE** takes the bundle into his hands. He stiffens, holding the baby out in front of him.)*

(...)

*(He pulls **WALKING MAN** in, cradling him with his arms.)*

(And he smiles.)

(It's a smile that could warm a hundred winters...)

(And it will.)

(...)

*(**EARLY** puts the truck in gear.)*

End of Play

www.ingramcontent.com/pod-product-compliance
Lightning Source LLC
LaVergne TN
LVHW011300180925
821343LV00033B/700